Assignment—

—Tiger Devil

Will B. Aarons

A FAWCETT GOLD MEDAL BOOK

Fawcett Publications, Inc., Greenwich, Connecticut

ASSIGNMENT TIGER DEVIL

© 1977 FAWCETT PUBLICATIONS, INC.
ALL RIGHTS RESERVED

ISBN 0–449–13811–9

Printed in the United States of America

10 9 8 7 6 5 4 3 2 1

Chapter One

Durell spoke above the night chant of insects and frogs down below on the jungled bank of the Demerara River. "You're sure Dick said the binnacle?"

"It was his last word to me," Peta said.

His last word on earth, Durell thought.

He glanced about the rusty wheelhouse of the *Peerless,* cocked an ear. "Can you see anything on the foredeck?"

"No. Hurry." Tension rasped in the voice of the half-French, half-Arawak Indian youth.

"I heard something."

"I'd hear it before you," Peta said.

"You may know the sounds of the forest, but I know the sounds of men," Durell said.

It did not surprise him that someone else was at the darkened wreck. After Boyer, he would be next on the murderer's list, of coursé.

Durell listened again, his electric torch lying beside his knee. A motorboat frog puttered, down among the anacondas and cayman alligators. There was the tireless stirring of the tradewind through crowns of mangrove and white cedar, manni and crabtree, as it cooled the Atlantic shore of tropical Guyana. Through the broken windows of the wheelhouse came a stench compounded of bog and decay, the watery overscent of the thrusting river that had lured Sir Walter Raleigh toward a mythical El Dorado.

Durell forced an impatient breath through his nostrils, and said: "It's no use. All the screws are frozen in place. Dick couldn't have hidden anything here. The binnacle hasn't been touched in years."

"Keep looking." Peta's hand suddenly held a flat-barreled pistol, a Chinese-made Tokarev. Stamped ideograms glinted under its slide grip. It hung loosely at his side, its muzzle pointed at the floor, and Durell did not know if he showed it as a threat.

"Where did you get that?" he said.

"Mr. Boyer had it when he died."

Durell wondered if the boy lied.

"Put it away, kid," he said.

"I'm not a kid."

The boy was seventeen at most. Back home he'd be out on a date or studying his lessons, instead of hiring out as a guide.

Peta regarded Durell through fierce green eyes, and said: "I'm a man. I've been cut for hunting."

He offered a view of his upper right arm, and Durell saw scar welts. When the cuts were fresh, *beana,* a potion of herbs and animal bone, had been rubbed into them to bring good luck on the hunt. The boy was rangy as bushrope, almost as tall as Durell, maybe a fraction quicker of movement. But he lacked Durell's solid strength, his sureness and his combat instincts. He looked competent, considering his age, but his solitary thoughts, his intentions, his loyalties—all were question marks.

There were no dossiers on Peta Gibaudan; Durell doubted there was even a birth certificate.

He considered Peta through dark eyes that turned almost black, as they usually did when he was thoughtful or angry. He continued to monitor the night beyond the walls of the wheelhouse with senses honed by more years than he cared to remember as chief field agent for K Section, the troubleshooting arm of the CIA.

Peta might be trying to prove something about courage and manhood, but he had chosen the wrong time and place.

Or he might be a Judas goat, leading him to the slaughter.

Either way, he was a dangerous liability now, Durell decided. "Want me to take that gun away from you?" he said.

"I only want to help, Mr. Durell. You said someone

6

was out there." Peta's coppery face looked uncertain, his eyes offended, above sharp cheekbones. The torch on the floor made a pond of radiance that oiled beaded bands the boy wore beneath his knees.

"Go back to the corial, the dugout canoe," Durell said.

"I'll stay here," Peta replied. Then he stiffened as the motorboat frog lapsed into frightened silence.

"Relax, son," Durell said. "Go back down the manni tree to old Thomas."

"You may need me," Peta said stubbornly.

"Get the hell out of here."

"All right. But I could help you." Peta thrust the 7.62mm into the pocket of his ragged khaki shorts, and his sneakers made a faint squelching sound as he turned and became a shadow moving through the door; then he was gone, silently.

Durell's eyes went to his wristwatch. Thirty-five minutes had elapsed. He was pressing his luck. He glanced beyond the shattered windscreen. There was no moon, but the starshine of equatorial South America gave some light. The old freighter was once a proud vessel of the Athel Line of London, to judge by remnants of its red and maroon paint. It had been beached when its cargo caught fire years ago, according to Peta, and had silted in and overgrown with jungle. It was difficult to discern anything on its gloomy deck.

Durell thought of a legend that might be fact, a murderously crazed presence that might be animal. Or man. Or nothing.

The Warakabra Tiger.

A chill stole into his chest, and he looked away from the eerie darkness and turned back to his task.

Again he went over each detail of the binnacle: magnet chamber, quadrantal spheres, compass hood. The wheelhouse was dank and warm. Sweat rolled off the tip of his nose as he probed the mute steel and brass, chafed at his paucity of information.

Neither General Dickinson McFee, his gray little boss at K Section, nor Chad Mitchell, his liaison with the embassy in Georgetown, had been very helpful.

And on the old *Peerless*, Durell did not even know what it was he sought.

He raised the torch, aware of the increased risk that it might be seen. A bauxite freighter's horn sounded on the Demerara. A turboprop approaching Timehri Airport whined over centuries-old graves of Dutchmen on abandoned river plantations. Durell's attention was caught by a needle of reflection.

He thrust the light closer to the compass card and saw among a tangle of spider webs that must have been broken by Dick Boyer's hand a small, linear scratch. It ended at the edge of the gimbaled card, pointing across the bridge toward an empty shelf that was waist-high on the wall.

A thud of footsteps came from below.

Durell was blinded by an afterglow of floating golf-ball images as he doused the light. He wondered if Peta were safely off the ship. There had been no cries of alarm, no sounds of struggle. Anxiety grappled against his control as he went swiftly to the shelf, ran fingers back and forth under it. They touched a hard nodule, held there by tree gum. He snatched it loose, dropped it into his trousers pocket and slid toward the door, just as a hollow chime of feet reached the top of the steel ladder outside.

He did not wait, but jerked the door open on a man bent forward with caution and slammed the heavy torch into his face.

Shards rattled from the splintered lens, and the man toppled backward and cascaded down the metal steps with a long rumble. His automatic weapon clanked against the deck, went off with a burp of automatic fire that drew scolding shrieks from howler monkeys. Durell cursed the racket and hurled himself down the ladder two, three steps at a time, eyes on the port quarter of the fantail.

There came a confusion of shouts as men rounded the superstructure.

Durell jumped over the dark heap lying at the foot of the ladder, darted for the stern. His soles thudded urgently against the deckplates, and the tradewind bellied his white worsted jacket behind him. His thick, black hair was

8

tinged with gray at the temples, but he moved with the lithe efficiency of a college sprinter.

He felt a thump as a slug smashed against the heel of his right shoe.

Submachine guns yammered; bright pips of lead burst on the railing toward which he reached.

And then he was falling, falling . . .

Chapter Two

McFee's call had come the previous afternoon at Deirdre Padgett's rose-brick colonial house near Washington, D.C. Durell's skipjack, a Chesapeake Bay oyster boat converted to a roomy pleasure sailer, had just been secured after a cruise south to Hampton Roads. The waters had been lulling, forgetful; the long nights filled with lovemaking.

Durell waited for Deirdre on the terrace in the shade of big old elms and oaks. A mockingbird was singing. Seen far beyond the small, weathered boat shed down by the beach, a fleet of Lightnings raced. Their white sails mimicked small clouds above the blue-and-silver-streaked water.

Here, a mile from Prince John, Maryland, was Durell's Eden. In a world he had traversed time and again, there was only one other place where he felt at home, the old beached sidewheeler, *Trois Belles*. His grandpa Jonathan, one of the last of the Mississippi River gamblers, had brought him to maturity there, teaching him the secrets of the Louisiana bayous and of why men gambled and why they lost. But Durell returned to the Bayou Pêche Rouge even less frequently than to Prince John.

Durell would not have called himself a patriot, but he had willingly chosen to live his life on the dark, lonely fringe that was society's frontier against the barons of greed and power and conquest. He had found himself in the only arena left where a man's worth might be judged in large measure by a silent move, an efficient kill. He had become ruthlessly competent—and increasingly aware that luck was a wild mare he must ride, but could never bridle.

A screen door banged and Deirdre brought a pitcher of ice and Durell's favorite bourbon toward the wrought-iron table. "You look tired," she said, and her oval face glowed mischievously. "Maybe last night taught you a lesson about staying away from me too long, darling."

"It taught me something I'd like to repeat right now."

"Be serious, Sam. You're not fully recovered from Lebanon."

He turned his dark eyes toward the Lightnings and made no reply. He had no wish to think about that slaughterhouse now. She stood beside him, and he felt her hand smooth the back of his head, as she said, "I wish you hadn't renewed your contract."

"It was due to expire this week, Dee."

"But you could have postponed it; had a real vacation. McFee would take you back when you were good and ready. He says you should listen to him and take that desk in Analysis and Synthesis. He says—"

"I know. The computer puts my survival factor at next to nothing."

"Why must you continue to tempt fate, darling Sam?"

He turned his eyes up to where the radiance of the sky brought out the copper sheen of her raven hair. "I'm doing what I'm best suited for," he said.

He slid his hands around her waist, and his fingertips almost touched. There had been other women, but when they were together, he had no thought of anyone else. She was the only perfect woman for Durell. His fingers moved down the slope of her drillcloth shorts.

Her smile was warm and serene, and there was wonder and love in her intelligent gray eyes. "Do you want to?" she asked. "It's only three in the afternoon."

"Say goodnight to the mockingbird," he said. He stood

and realized again how tall she was. Her lips met his eagerly.

The telephone rang.

"Don't answer it," she said.

"Dee—"

"Don't, Sam. It's McFee. I know it."

Durell found the telephone on a Sheraton cabinet next to a bow window.

"Samuel?" Only McFee called him that.

"Yes, sir?"

"Let's go to scramble."

Durell flicked a switch at the back of the cabinet, and heard McFee say: "Richard Boyer is dead. Murdered." McFee rarely showed emotion, and did not now. He abhorred it as counterproductive. Durell sometimes wondered if he were capable of feeling anything.

"Where, sir?" Durell swallowed.

"Guyana. He was Georgetown control—I thought he was a close friend of yours." McFee's voice remained precise, businesslike.

"He was. Same class at Yale and at The Farm. We've been out of touch a couple of years." Durell thought of Dick's wife, the two sons he and Dick had taught to sail on the Severn River. He said, "Has Marie been told?"

"Strand is on his way to deliver the news now. He knows the family."

"How did it happen, sir?"

"Shot in the back. We know very little else. Boyer hadn't filed a Field Information Report in some time. A Georgetown newspaper blew his cover in a front-page story two days ago. Some anti-American hothead apparently read it and decided to settle the CIA's hash on the spot."

"What's been done about it so far?"

"The police are investigating, of course. Our ambassador has been assured that the murderer will be brought to justice. Chad Mitchell of the embassy staff will interview the embassy's employees in hopes of finding out who leaked the information, but it's not likely we'll ever know—probably a Guyanese who thought he was being patriotic."

There was a pause. The song of the mockingbird came through the windowpanes. Then Durell said: "I'd like to go down there, sir."

"I thought you would."

Durell's voice was bitter as he said: "Dick might still be alive if the newspaper hadn't printed that story."

"I understand your drift. I must caution you that K Section is most hesitant to cause trouble with the media. If you do, Western Hemisphere Division will have your head— not to mention State."

"The reporter knows who put the finger on Dick, sir."

"You're not to molest the reporter, Samuel. We don't want the negative publicity it could cause. We're embarrassed enough over the public disclosure of Boyer."

"Dick would regret that his death has embarrassed you, sir."

"Now, Samuel, the guidelines come straight from Sugar Cube. We must be discreet. The government of Guyana will not take kindly to our interference in their police matters. If you take the assignment, you'll operate as Dick's brother-in-law, going down to wind up his affairs. And you will stay clear of the homicide investigation."

"And my hands will be tied, so that diplomats can still smile at each other over cocktails." Durell might easily have spoken in anger, but his voice was thoughtful.

"You may refuse the mission," McFee said.

"I'll go, despite the prohibitions." Durell's tone became blunt. "Now tell me the real objective of the assignment. It goes deeper than Boyer's murder, doesn't it, sir."

"Perhaps Boyer's murder is as simple as it seems—"

"But you don't think so."

"I'm merely reserving judgment. Have you ever heard of an animal called the Warakabra Tiger?"

"Only vaguely, as a myth out of the rain forests."

"Some Guyanese claim it really exists. I had Research look into it."

The phone brought a shuffling of papers, and Durell visualized McFee, in impeccable gray suit and dark gray tie, secreted in his fortress quarters atop K Section headquarters near Washington's Diplomats' Row. Close at hand would be his ever-present blackthorn walking stick with its hidden implements of death.

McFee said: "It is described as a wolf-size cat that runs in packs. It literally tears up the forest floor in a voracious frenzy, uprooting seedlings and saplings, ripping the bark off larger trees, leaving swaths of destruction twenty to thirty feet wide. No one knows what sends it on these rampages—if it exists. The devastation has been verified by respected authorities, but there isn't a single eyewitness account of the packs themselves."

There came a pause. Durell waited, aware that McFee was leading up to something.

Then McFee continued: "Communications picked up an emergency transmission from Boyer four nights ago. It was very poor quality, as if his equipment were damaged or the batteries had deteriorated. He did not respond to a request for a repeat. We got something on tape: two words. Warakabra and tiger."

"If Dick broke in on the Q channel, it wasn't to describe the local fauna," Durell said. "Have the lab boys tried enhancement?"

"Every process known to man, Samuel. The transmission was simply too weak. The tape has given us all we'll get. It's enough to make me suspect that something of the gravest consequence is afoot down there."

"I'll find out what it is, sir."

"Keep in mind that Guyana is a small sliver stuck in the shoulder of South America, that if the wrong hands held it, it could become a wedge into the vitals of Brazil and Venezuela, the mineral-rich keystones to a stable continent."

"I'm aware of that."

"You needn't delay your departure; I've given you all the information we have."

"Very well, sir."

There was a click. The line went dead.

The Chesapeake seemed smug, contemptuous of Durell and all mortality. Deirdre waited beside the white iron table, gray eyes determinedly calm. When she saw his expression, she averted her face.

He spoke gently. "It's Dick Boyer, Dee. A homicide in Guyana."

"Dick?" She buried her face in her hands.

Durell waited. A Niarchos tanker churned down from Baltimore, its yellow funnel a lily on the great gray box of its hull. Seagulls circled and dipped in its wake. It was not the first time he'd had to tell Deirdre of the death of a dear and mutual friend. She'd always found an accepting courage. He hoped it would serve her as well when another might bring her such word about him. Countless men would pay any price for his head; his dossiers had been red-tabbed by the Soviet KGB and Peking's Black House, and they were patient and thorough organizations. The red tabs meant simply that he was marked to die. Deirdre knew it as well as he. She played relentlessly at forgetting it. He could not afford to.

She looked at him through wet eyes. "I'm sorry, darling. Forgive me. It must be worse for you."

"I'm going to Guyana," he said.

"Of course. When?"

"Immediately."

"I'll go with you."

"No."

"You said I did well that time in Thailand."

"I can't risk you, Dee, even if McFee would allow it." He took her in his arms and kissed her tenderly.

She caught her breath as their lips parted. "Sam, darling, sometimes I feel that our life together is an enormous bank account that we can draw on only in small change, an hour here, a day there."

"I'm sorry." He broke away and strode down the brick walk to his old Chevrolet. "Be here for me when I get back?" he called.

"Always," she said.

Chapter Three

Durell boarded a 5:30 commuter flight to Kennedy, then a BOAC 707 from New York direct to Guyana. It was shortly after midnight when he arrived.

Chad Mitchell met him at Timehri International Airport twenty-five miles south of Georgetown. The steam one breathed for air here smelled ripely of the jungle that was all around. Chad was a brusque man with a yellow mat of oiled hair and moody brown eyes. His tan, tropical-weight suit was slightly rumpled, as if he had worked in it all day, and he looked tired and smoked too many cigarettes. He had begun his career with K Section back in the '60s, put in five years in Latin America and managed to pull strings to get switched to State and the Foreign Service. He hoped to win an ambassadorship someday. At the moment, he handled commercial affairs for Guyana and, because of his background, internal security for the embassy.

"Damned sorry business; hope you can wrap it up quickly. Never thought embassy security would amount to anything; now my whole schedule has gone down the chute. Had to cancel a meeting with the Alcoa people today. God damn it."

"Most vexing," Durell said.

"You work your ass off, and what do you get?"

"Constipated."

"Don't be funny, Sam."

"I mean if it doesn't grow back. You really have a problem, Chad."

They drove in silence as the land opened onto canefields and coconut plantations. This was one of the few paved highways in the country, and the embassy Lincoln purred hungrily at the chance for a workout. Then they passed a sugar refinery and Radio Demerara and were in the sprawling wooden mix of Georgian to Victorian buildings that constituted most of Georgetown. Guyana was the size of Idaho, its population roughly equivalent to that of Indianapolis. A fourth of its people lived in the capital city, mixed together rich and poor where the original slave plantations had been subdivided and shanty patches sprung up among barnlike white manor houses and tossing palms. The sullen night was charged with expectancy. Durell sensed that almost anything could happen here.

Finally, Chad said: "Dick had gone downhill since his glory days in the Far East. He blundered away his cover and paid the price. That news story was an invitation to murder for every kook in Guyana. I really don't know why you're here, Sam."

"You're not expected to. Where did they find Dick's body?"

"An Indian kid notified the police early Sunday morning. Said the man came there half-dead, expired on the porch. The kid tried to help him; didn't know what to do, of course."

"Did Dick tell him anything?"

Chad shook his head and blew out cigarette smoke. "He's just a bushboy."

"What's his name?"

"Peta Gibaudan. Peta's an Amerindian name. But he's half-French."

Durell cracked a window to let some cigarette smoke escape the air-conditioned car. "I'll want to talk with him."

"No idea what took Dick there. He hadn't logged in at the embassy for almost a week, but he was gone often. No one thought much about it."

"He always kept his own counsel."

"Poor procedure," Chad said.

Durell watched the colonial-pink parliament building glide past, then the concrete and half-timbered Victoria Law Courts, shorn since independence of the dumpy statue of its namesake. "Don't take me to my hotel just yet," he said. "Let's go to the morgue."

"What for? Don't start making a case that doesn't exist. The police think the killer was an East Indian, acting alone. The ambassador's convinced, and he doesn't want you pushing anybody around. We've enough problems here—you know the East Indians never forgave the CIA for knocking their Marxist leader out of the prime minister's office with those labor riots in the '60s." Chad sighed wearily as his yellow fingers crumpled a cigarette butt in the ashtray, and said: "Just discuss it with the ambassador, Sam. Write your report and wrap it up."

"I want to see Dick's body."

"If you insist. First thing in the morning." Chad twisted the wheel and they turned past the Bank of Guyana Building, then to the right, down Main Street.

"Tonight. Now." Durell's tone was stubborn.

"The morgue's closed."

"Get it opened. Wake the ambassador."

Chad's brown eyes widened. "He's been asleep two hours. It wouldn't be wise."

"Wake him up."

Chad did not bother to conceal the contempt in his voice as he said: "Dick was your pal, so you see this as the beginning of World War III."

The smell of formaldehyde and antiseptics and death pinched Durell's nose. Chad made a grimace of distaste as a little African attendant took away the shroud. The black police sergeant who had escorted them here on special orders was impassive.

Minutely, Durell regarded the long, white body. It did not look like Dick, was thin and disproportionately aged. Random bruises and bloodless scratches marred the flesh from thin, sandy hair to stiffened yellow toes.

"He didn't get those bruises and lacerations sitting around Georgetown," Durell said. His voice echoed in the barren room. "He must have spent some time in the forest. Look at his feet." He pointed to where the skin

17

was blotched and blistered by damp and fungus and hard use.

"I don't know that it means anything," Chad said.

"Your duty is a sad one," said the white-clad attendant. His face wore a sorrowful smile. "Of course, I see death every night. It is my job. Eleven to seven."

Durell's eyes continued to scour the wasted flesh. He had not moved from his place at the head of the enameled table.

"When I go home to my wife and children in the Werken-Rust District, do they ask how was my work? They never mention it. It is like eleven to seven does not exist, only what happens the rest of the time. But eleven to seven is what I think about the rest of the time."

"I've known others with similar problems," Durell said. He moved to the end of the table near the feet.

"What did they do about it?" The little man leaned against the table and it rolled an inch.

"They keep going, until they die."

"You're thinking about your poor brother-in-law, yes? He had a job that weighed on his mind?"

Durell said nothing.

Chad said: "Are you finished? Are you satisfied? I'll have enough trouble sleeping as it is. The ambassador was really teed off."

Durell indicated a large, discolored carbuncle on the calf of the corpse. "Why didn't they get this out?" he said. He turned to Chad. "Further confirmation of a stay in the jungle."

The attendant peered at the nodule and curled his nose. "Ah, the seeka worm is dead, sir. At any rate, the dead man no longer feels it. Shall I lance it, sir?"

"Don't bother."

"I will," the black man insisted.

"Leave him alone." Durell allowed his eyes to rove to a small blue exit hole under the sixth rib. A lung shot.

The African followed Durell's gaze, and said: "He bled to death. The wound might not have been fatal, if he'd received treatment."

Durell thought of Marie and the children. "Where's the wedding ring?" he asked.

"Oh!" The attendant went briskly to a cabinet and withdrew a paper bag. "Wedding ring, wristwatch, wallet," he said. He gave a satisfied smile and handed the brown bag to Durell.

Durell crumpled it into his jacket pocket, as his gaze lingered briefly on the sunken eyes of the body. The closed lids looked as if they had been dusted with pencil lead. More real than grief was a feeling of loss. The mathematical logic of K Section's computer was justified again—and the old hands continued to die violently.

He felt an emptiness around him.

A gulf of time and history was between him and most of those on the roster now.

He walked to the door and nodded over his shoulder at the corpse. "Put it in a box," he said.

Durell paused on the wooden steps outside the morgue. Houses and trees blocked the tradewind, and the air was humid and heavy. Fog crept out of a canal across the street. He took a deep breath, cut his eyes up and down the avenue, saw no sign of surveillance. Worry gnawed under his ribs, as he strode to the car.

"The ambassador thinks a public show of grief is important—he wants a ceremony tomorrow," Chad said.

"The hypocritical bastard," Durell said.

"Better be there—you're the brother-in-law, remember?"

"Oh, hell," Durell said.

Chad waited impatiently as Durell checked into his hotel, then drove him to the embassy at 31 Main Street. Durell glimpsed a big crepe bow on the front door, as Chad escorted him past a Marine guard and into a side entrance. Dick's cubbyhole office was in the basement, out of sight and hearing of anything else, behind double steel doors with all the standard entry prevention and detection devices of K Section Controls worldwide.

"If you get in there, you'll be the first one besides Dick to see what it's like," Chad said.

"I'll get in. Go home and get some sleep."

"I've come this far; might as well hang around. Want some coffee?"

"No, thanks. You'll have to leave, Chad."

"Well, I was with you guys for five years, for chrissakes."

"You're not with us now."

Chad would have been disappointed, Durell thought as he opened the door and turned on a ceiling light. The small, sparsely furnished office was out of the ordinary only in the immediate chill of its air-conditioning vent, the first on a conduit from the embassy's big cooling plant. There was a small steel desk with a picture of Marie and the boys; an electric typewriter with a stroke powerful enough to cut FIR mats; a wooden console of modern design with a hot plate and kettle for steaming letters open or making instant coffee; and enormous maps on two walls, one of Guyana and another of South America. Against a flimsy partition sat two six-drawer filing cabinets with combination locks. In them were logs, field reports, dossiers and dated lists of noteworthy passengers into and out of the country, obtained from airline and shipping sources. On the other side of the partition were a transmitter, receiver and encoding machine. Code discs and books were in a steel safe, where the wrong touch would ignite incinerating Thermit bombs.

Durell took off his jacket, rinsed a cup, put water on to boil and started with the top drawer of the first filing cabinet.

He paused only once, about four AM, to call Chad, who was less than pleased.

"You know Phil Gordon, the Toepfer Motors distributor here?"

"Yes."

"Good. I want you to give him a call for me."

"Now? Call him yourself."

Durell was tired, and his nerves were strained, and he gripped the phone very tightly, as he said in a low, even voice: "Chad, I don't like reminding you that you're under my orders. You know this man, so the chances of cooperation are better."

"What do you want me to tell him?" Chad grumbled.

"He's our cutout to Calvin Wilfred Eisler; get him to set up a meeting with Eisler for me."

"Dick had Calvin Eisler on his string? The national assemblyman? Jesus. And old Phil, too."

"Maybe Dick was sharper than you gave him credit for," Durell said. The files Durell had just read showed that Eisler was one of Dick Boyer's best sources. He was a member of one of the few aristocratic families remaining in Guyana and received a regular subsidy from K Section. Most significant, he was the only person mentioned in Dick's files or logbook in connection with the Warakabra Tiger.

Durell worked through Dick's data, sorting, sifting, weighing and memorizing, for two more hours. Then he strolled back to his hotel through a clown-colored dawn and fell into an exhausted sleep.

Chapter Four

That afternoon they held the brief farewell ceremony. Dick's flag-draped casket was on the lawn of the embassy, a block from the stellings of the river. The sun's yellow heat pressed against the neatly clipped grass and weighed down the leaves of purple-flowered bougainvillaea and eucalyptus trees.

Durell, at the edge of the small gathering, scanned youths who lounged about the wallaba-wood telephone poles and shoppers with packages under their arms. A disorderly stream of cars, yellow buses and mule carts clattered and roared on Main Street. The street was divided by a strip of lawn and flamboyant trees clustered with brilliant red blossoms. Small knots of Africans and East Indians, a sprinkling of Chinese and Caucasian faces watched from their shade.

Sparkling cumulus clouds gathered above the muddy Atlantic to the north, preparing an assault over the ancient seawall that kept the city and much of the densely inhabited coastal strip from flooding. The air was gloomy beneath their violet undersides.

It was not difficult to spot Otelo Antunes. Just to be sure, Durell lifted a brow toward Chad, and Chad nodded affirmation.

Otelo's by-line had been over the story that revealed Dick's connection with the CIA.

The dark Portuguese, clad in loose-tailed white shirt and blue trousers, stood beside the hearse, ballpoint pen poised over a stenographer's pad. His lips were tight and rejecting on an ascetic face, but the black eyes were ravenous. His whiplike frame seemed built for squeezing under doors, his pale hands startlingly big and grasping.

He returned Durell's gaze with a willful stare.

Durell clenched his fists in his pockets, as the ambassador's comments droned on.

The squall line hit with a gale that flung surprised herons and street trash toward the rum shops on Water Street. The wind blew away the ambassador's words, and the gathering stirred on the verge of breaking up. A page of the *Evening Post*, competitor to Otelo's *Guyana Sentinel*, flopped and spun toward Durell and clung against his leg. He peeled it loose and saw a story announcing dedication soon of a new dam constructed deep in the interior by the People's Republic of China. The prime minister of the Cooperative Republic of Guyana would attend.

Lightning banged. A white storm of raindrops lashed the street as the coffin was rushed to the rear of the hearse, red and white stripes sagging wetly down its sides. The crowd ran for cover.

Durell yelled to Chad and they jumped into a yellow

Fiat he had rented at Ramahan's Esso Station, opposite Stabroek Market. He did not see where Otelo went.

He wiped water from his face and cursed softly and decided Otelo could wait.

"What about Eisler?" he asked.

"I alerted the cutout. He hasn't been able to reach him," Chad said.

"Did you try to contact Eisler directly? Every hour counts."

"We have to maintain some discretion, Sam."

"To hell with it; I'll go to him myself."

"I advise against it. You may blow a good agent."

"He's no good if he doesn't help us now."

"He's got his career to think about, damn it. If it gets out he's worked for us, the scandal will ruin him. Give him some time—"

"I can't afford to wait."

"It's on your own head." Chad sounded angry.

"That's where it usually is," Durell replied.

Chad slammed the car door and ran through the rain into the embassy. Durell headed out of town to find the mud-trash shack of Peta Gibaudan.

Peta's coppery face showed suspicion of Durell, and he came reluctantly out of the undergrowth that surrounded his stilted house. He carried a *warishi* rucksack of Amerindian basketwork behind his naked shoulders. The head of a pheasantlike maroudi swung from it. His hands held a wicked-looking twelve-gauge shotgun of ancient manufacture.

The police and Americans had asked too many questions, he said. He wanted to answer no more. Still, Durell correctly judged that Peta relished an occasional visitor no less than others who spent much of their lives in the solitary backwaters of the world. Durell just sat quietly on the splintery steps of the porch and watched as Peta squatted, gutted the bird efficiently and tossed its entrails into the turbid river.

Durell bided his time, as Peta roasted the bird. Peta paid him no attention. The aroma of an open fire and sizzling fat filled the air. Then Peta lifted the fowl on its spit and, careful not to burn his fingers, twisted off a leg and shoved it at Durell. "Here. Maroudi is good," he said.

The flesh was light and tasty, slightly gamy, and Durell thought of wild turkeys he had roasted as a boy in the Louisiana parishes.

They finished the meal as, with tropical abruptness, the sun pulled the vermilion-tinged gold of daylight's awning beneath the horizon. Peta sat on the porch, licking his fingers like a cat, and still they did not talk. Then Peta moved away through the darkness and returned with a gallon jug of high wine—rum straight from the distillery, in which a beefsteak had been suspended for a few days to soak up the acetone and fusel oil.

It was pepper on the tongue and lay in the stomach like a wad of hot nettles.

Finally, Durell tried once more. "Tell me about Dick, Peta. It's very important. What happened here?"

Peta's green eyes regarded him thoughtfully, then he spoke slowly, telling how the man had stumbled out of the forest and collapsed on the porch where they sat. "I tried to help him, but he died. He was my friend."

"Your friend?" Durell put a hand on the youth's shoulder. "You did all you could," he said.

Peta's black hair shimmered iridescently as he shook his head. "No. I boiled trysil bark for a poultice to stop the bleeding. I should have run for help."

"It was too late; he was dead on his feet. I've had to leave men like that behind. At least Dick didn't have to die alone."

Peta looked down at the hands clasped between his banded calves.

"Which way did he come from?" Durell asked.

"Downstream." Peta pointed toward Georgetown. Durell was surprised, since he had supposed that Dick came from the interior.

"And you heard nothing? No shots?"

"No." Peta hesitated. "But he told me something. It puzzles me. I've kept it quiet, but you are not with the authorities; you are his relative."

Gently, Durell prodded: "What, Peta?"

"He said binnacle. That was all. What does it mean?"

"It's part of a ship, the post that holds the compass. Do you know what ship he could have been talking about?"

Then Peta told him of the old wreck of the *Peerless*, not far downriver, and Durell thought it plausible. Dick had had a lifelong romance with boats and ships, and his curiosity might have taken him to the *Peerless* many times.

"I know nothing of ships," Peta said. "Tell me how to find the binnacle."

"Take me there. I'll find it," Durell said.

Chapter Five

Durell was suspended among the branches of the manni tree, down beside the hull of the *Peerless*. Words from across a numbed distance snaked through the broken crockery of consciousness, worried his comprehension.

"Mr. Durell?"

He could not open his eyes, or, he thought in confusion, he was blind.

The words came again: "Mr. Durell?"

The world heaved on springs and was smothered in a vile odor of slime. His lips tried to articulate something as he groped toward an inferno that roared at the back of his head, where a bullet must have clipped his skull. The momentum of his dash from the wheelhouse had carried him over the ship's rail. It came back to him as a dream of anxiety that he might have had hours or only seconds ago.

He felt a hand dig roughly into his jacket, remembered vaguely the heavy lump in his trousers pocket. Sight returned dimly, and the sky blinked at him through the canopy of the tree. Swirly star-banners. A shaggy-haired form.

Peta labored through another of Durell's jacket pockets. Instead of returning to the corial, he had waited at the tree they had climbed to board the hulk.

Now he wanted what Durell had found—

A pounding chattering and muzzle flame erupted from the ship's rail, where someone fired blindly into the foliage, not knowing if Durell was dead or alive, hoping to finish him with wild shots.

When it stopped, Peta was gone. Durell could only wonder if the youth had fled or been shot out of the tree. There came a raw stench of gunpowder over the reek of primal mud and decay. The teeming Demerara was a powerful murmur a few yards away, and a foghorn sounded from a humid distance where its mouth was Georgetown's harbor. Durell shielded a penflash with his body as he studied the object taken from the wheelhouse. Flaky brown vegetable residue clung to it, and he rubbed it away to reveal a lightly pitted stone.

It was a diamond.

A raw diamond the size of a prune.

He heard a command, and a rope ladder slapped down the side of the ship. It was no surprise that the command was in English. The language of Guyana's last colonial masters was the national tongue for descendants of African slaves and of imported plantation laborers, Portuguese from Madeira, Hindus and Moslems from India, Chinese.

Durell reached out hurriedly, gripped a thick limb and worked toward the center of the tree until he found the liana-webbed trunk. A hairy something scuttered across the back of his hand, and he jerked back, almost falling. There were tarantulas here that grew six inches across. He wiped sweat from his eyesockets, as his thudding heart rapped against the wound at the back of his head. Then he hung from a low branch and dropped into the muck. The light splash was lost in a cacophony of insect and toad voices.

26

There was no sign of Peta in the sprangled vegetation.

Durell had only one thought in mind, and that was to get away from the ship before the men could reach him.

Boots scraped and thudded down the hull plates, off to his left. In moments the jungle would be rife with armed men—as it already was with lethal spiders and scorpions, alligators, perhaps a jaguar.

He hoped that Peta had not already taken the corial. The Demerara was a mile wide here. With battering rafts of flotsam swept down from the rain forests, tricky currents and deadly predators, it was nearly impossible to swim.

He kept his snub-nosed .38 Smith and Wesson Special in its holster and dived into the foliage, bearing north. He'd need both hands to tear his way through, and then he'd be lucky if he got very far.

Mud sucked at his feet, shaggy lianas enmeshed him, vampire bats fluttered through the branches—the natives called them "Dr. Moses," he remembered, after an old physician notorious a century before for bleeding his patients. The mosquito-borne diseases of malaria and yellow fever had been stamped out, but many inhabitants still slept under netting for safety from the vampires. Durell sensed things slithering and crawling, as the men stirred up monkeys and labbas and God only knew what else in their search of the swampy brush. Their lights washed and winked and splattered into coins of radiance on knife-edged awaraballi palms, and when they called to each other, their voices were muffled in the black hell.

Durell stayed close to the riverbank. It was madness to stray far from the Demerara, since most of the country was uninhabited and unexplored. Only swamps, bloated rivers and rain forests stretched for hundreds of miles in a titanic wilderness.

He tripped over the loop of a manni root, struggled from one handhold to the next as heart-shaped caladiums slapped him and prickly bactris fronds tore at his clothing. Every leaf spilled a measure of water, and he was soaking, and his breath shouted in his ears.

It had been easy, going to the *Peerless*. Peta had

searched out a deer track with flagrant skill, but Durell now failed to pick it up, was unsure of its location.

His pursuers had fanned out; some could have passed him and doubled back. Like the bushmasters and coral snakes, one might strike at any time.

Suddenly he broke into a tree-vaulted space where a stream ran through. He glanced about, felt a tremor of relief. This was the small cove in which the corial had been hidden. He called softly for Peta, aware of yellow beams of light that rippled overhead, the dim slosh of boots as the men approached from behind.

Peta made no reply.

He risked a second hoarse whisper, this time for Thomas, the grizzled old boatman who had ferried them across with his ten-horse outboard.

There was no response.

The water was warm as he waded in an ankle-deep stew of algae, bending toward the river through undergrowth, spreading fronds and twigs as he went. The stream widened to a glistening stage with curtains of foliage hanging in the flies.

The black length of the corial sat like a coffin washed up by the current. Durell rushed to shove it off and saw that it *was* a coffin of sorts.

Old Thomas lay dead in there.

The dim shape of his body sprawled on the bottom, mouth open in death-awe, eyes glittery against his black face. Durell questioned the killer's presence with a glance to right and left, saw nothing, pushed again, and the boat broke loose from the sucking mud. As he waded after it, the cove was a welter of smells, overripe hog plums, figs, swamp gas, bush cow droppings.

He heard the men distinctly now. But for the dugout, they would have trapped him against the stream. Urgently he threw a knee over the boat's gunwale—and a low rattle of droplets sounded at his back.

His belly went cold as he twisted just in time to block a naked forearm and deflect the wet flash of a knife. Instinct rammed signals through his nerves as the knife looped back toward his spleen. He caught the knife hand, rammed his knee in the direction of a groin that was a guess in the ebony shadows. He missed and lost his footing, and his face hit the tepid water as the other's knee thudded hard between his shoulder blades. A brutal hand clutched his hair, pushing him down. Durell clamped his lips against the sour water, hung onto the knife hand and heaved, struggling for a foothold on the yielding bottom sands.

The man held him under with a bullish strength, but could not shake his knife hand free of Durell's grip.

Durell's lungs began to burn.

He grabbed an ankle and felt the man totter, lifted the leg with all his muscle and crashed his head into the man's abdomen. The man stumbled back, still clinging to Durell's hair, trying to hold him under, and Durell had only a fraction of a second to exploit his advantage.

He reached up and around, fingers sliding over a rubber wetsuit, and grabbed heavy airtanks and wrenched the man over onto his back. Durell's mouth came out of the water with a taste of scum, and he twisted the man's arm and ground the knife between his ribs. Flippered feet thrashed into the air, and hands floundered whitely. There was a gargled scream. Durell plunged the blade into the frogman's heart.

Durell swayed, snorted the foul jungle soup from his nose.

His breath caught in his throat as he felt the water vibrate with movement, and he reached the stream bank in three crashing strides.

Piranhas.

One of the short, silver brutes came out with him, teeth clamped fanatically in his thigh. Durell cut it loose with the knife.

They rioted over the corpse, frenzied the surface of the creek where the corial drifted hopelessly beyond reach.

The men shouted from scant yards away, and Durell knew they had heard the commotion. All he could do was swim the stream or the river—and the stream was out of the question. He ran for the river and almost fell over something black and pliant—the frogman's rubber boat, tucked among mangrove roots.

He gave a brief thought to Peta, perhaps wounded, hidden in some tangled thicket, then clenched his lips and shoved the little raft onto the swift waters.

Long seconds passed as he paddled furiously, eyes on a black line that was the far shore, but there were no shots. No boats followed him.

The river was milky under the stars, overlain with chill vapors and vegetable odors. Its roiling current bore mats and rafts of tangled logs, lianas, seed pods, blossoms— then something more.

It came ominously out of the low, thin mist, its bow wave a trembling, shining thunder. The enormous steel whaleback of its hull passed on a ripping slur of turbulence.

A submarine.

With little more than its great black sail above the surface, it surged toward the Atlantic.

Chapter Six

The rubber boat touched shore and Durell scrambled up the grassy face of a dike. He looked back, listened, did not know if the men were out on the river now or not. Inland was a field that glimmered with orange coals where leaves had been burned from sugarcane in preparation for the harvest. The smoke touched his nostrils with a sweet fragrance. House lights shone from the middle distance. A piccolo frog piped. A steady breeze chilled Durell through his soaked clothing, and he buttoned his coat and began walking.

The dike ended two miles upriver at the edge of the plantation country, an uncomfortable hike in squishy shoes and clinging trousers. There, among canted moorings and a weatherbeaten dock, was old Thomas' hovel. Durell's rental Fiat was parked behind it at the end of a red dirt road.

There was no sign that Peta had made it back here.

Durell dug a wad of mechanic's rags from the car trunk and hurriedly cleaned his .38 of corrosive moisture. He could field-strip the weapon blindfolded, if need be.

As he worked, he debated driving the mile or so to Peta's shack to see if he was there, but decided against it.

It was more important to get the big diamond safely stowed.

The Berbice Hotel was on High Street near the Victorian-Gothic-Rhenish Town Hall, an enormous building of gray weatherboard. Chad had wanted to put Durell up at the modern, white cube of the Hotel Tower, which looked like something imported from San Diego and was almost directly across Main Street from the embassy, but Durell had preferred the Berbice. He liked the distance it kept between him and the other Americans, and the shady saman trees that spread drifts of pink flowers on the lawn and the garden of cassias, plumbagos and jacarandas. It had the lazy elegance of bygone days, when travelers spoke of Georgetown as the loveliest city in the Caribbean.

The lobby was busy and so was the bar, where a gaggle of technocrats from African states, in town for an international forum of some kind, traded drinks with a North Korean and a Mao-jacketed Chinese from the PRC mission.

The government of Guyana took pride in its Third World status: a memorial to Mahatma Gandhi stood in the Promenade Gardens, and, at the Company Path Garden, over at the old Anglican Cathedral, there was a monument to the founders of the nonaligned movement: Nasser, Nkrumah, Nehru and Tito.

Durell asked the desk clerk if there were any messages for him, and the clerk, looking askance at his muddy clothing, stuck a finger into a pigeon hole and withdrew two slips of paper. One asked that Durell return a telephone call from Chad. The other, written in a looping, feminine hand, said: "Welcome to the Garden City—they like to call it that here. How about a drink for old time's sake? I'll be at the Toucan Patio until eleven or so." It was signed, "Ana."

Durell glanced at the gilded clock above the desk. It was almost ten.

He made his voice louder than normal, as he said, "I want this placed in the hotel safe." He dropped the big, dirty stone on the rosewood counter so that it bounced off and he had to pick it up from the floor. He hoped he was not too obvious. But you couldn't catch a fish if you didn't bait the hook.

The unquestioning clerk scooped the gem into a manila envelope, wrote Durell's name across it and disappeared behind a partition of key boxes. He returned a moment later and gave Durell a receipt.

Durell felt eyes all over him in the crowded lobby.

Durell inspected his room in detail, using all the standard procedures, but it had not been entered during his absence. No dust, no wrinkles, no pulled threads. Everything exactly in place. Then he went a step further, regarding the walls and ceiling with care. He found no damp or off-color daubs of paint and could conclude that no listening devices had been planted behind the plaster. Thankfully, Durell noted that his room was higher than any of the surrounding buildings, out of reach of snipers and sensitive sound-gathering equipment. High Street was quiet beyond the old-fashioned Demerara windows that were vertical louvers you could push out with a pole to catch the tradewind. Strollers took the air near the wooden, flying-buttressed bulk of St. George's Cathedral.

Durell showered the stench of the swamp away, applied antibiotic salve to the scalp wound and numerous small cuts and scratches and put on a fresh drip-dry seersucker suit. Then he dialed Chad's apartment.

"Where have you been?" The State man sounded tired and angry.

"We'll talk about it later."

"I hope you weren't bugging Calvin Eisler."

Durrell said nothing.

"It's better to go through channels. I tried to contact Eisler through his cutout all afternoon. Then about five o'clock, the goddamn cutout tells me he won't try to set us up with Eisler anymore. He's very tense, Sam. Very uptight."

"Do you think he spoke with Eisler?"

"I think so, but he won't admit it. I think Eisler put a chill on him." Durell heard a spewing sound, as Chad blew cigarette smoke on the mouthpiece. Chad said, "Listen. The ambassador's nervous, Sam. Eisler swings a hell of a lot of weight, and the ambassador feels we can't afford to alienate him."

Durell said: "The ambassador's nervous. I'll keep that in mind."

"Don't be sarcastic. Guys like you just don't live in the real world, that's all."

Durell made no reply. He said, "Did the technical interviews turn up anything?"

"They were negative—those that were administered. Almost half of the Guyanese employees of the embassy simply refused to submit to the polygraph. We couldn't force them."

Durell's voice sounded angry. "Then we just have to assume that embassy security is shot. Work on the theory that everything's bugged, photographed, compromised. Tell the ambassador to shut down communication of all classified matter until further notice."

"Isn't that a bit extreme?"

"Somebody told Otelo Antunes about Dick. You've got people who won't take a lie detector test, so it's only reasonable to initiate what countermeasures we can."

"All right. I just hope you're not overreacting." Chad's voice softened hopefully. "It would help if I could tell the ambassador what you've been up to."

"Would you believe I found a fabulous diamond, and saw an alien submarine on the Demerara?"

"Oh, shit. Go to hell." Chad hung up.

Chapter Seven

The Toucan Patio, on Orange Walk near Bourdo Market, had no toucans and was not a patio. It was a clapboard fortress against the climate, its walls riddled with latticework and lathe-turned grills and Demerara windows. A second-story veranda looked into fronds of young coconut palms, and, rising above an iron-frilled roofpeak, there was a wind tower where patrons could enjoy the evening breeze with their Russian Bear or Bookers' rum.

Durell parked the rental Fiat and waited for headlamps to go out in a steel-gray Volkswagen that stopped half a block behind. He could have eluded the tail easily enough, but had chosen not to. The street was wet, and the wind rattled the palm fronds and brought the smell of more rain to come. Durell entered the nightclub through a doorway with a Red Spot beverage sign hanging beside it. He asked for Ana Morera's table and was sent on a three-story climb up a dim and dingy staircase that spoke faintly to his nostrils of mildew and kitchen grease.

He wished there was another way down, but saw no evidence of one.

Either this was an off-night, or Ana was a prized customer: she had the top of the wind tower all to herself. Another possibility, Durell thought, was that she had arranged it that way.

She sat in the golden lamplight, a drink before her, a silver-tipped cigarette burning in an ashtray of Indian pottery. She did not face the entrance, and Durell had a moment to study the room from the shadows. The small space was floored with rush matting and enclosed on three sides by many-paned windows that were half-opened. On the fourth side was a wall of polished greenheart that bore trophy heads of five jaguars.

Then he moved into the room, and her oval face warmed as she saw him. He remembered the provocation of her small mouth, the determined brown eyes that might turn to melted caramel or reflect inner fires like brass before a fireplace. Her long black hair was skinned back in an enormous bun that emphasized the proud lift of her chin and made the stem of her neck seem fragile. The low cut of her simple black dress displayed a cleavage of breasts buoyant with youth.

Durell sat down without speaking, took the hand she languidly offered. It was cold, and he wondered if that were the shaved ice in her gin-and-it, or something else.

She smiled and said: "I've grown up since you last saw me. I'm a big girl now. Yes?"

"Only in the right places," Durell said.

Her eyes were amused, her manner competent beyond her years. Durell considered the change in her since her college days at American University, where she had received a *cum laude* degree in International Studies. Now she seemed even more sure of herself, if that were possible, vain with the unpredictable brilliance of Spanish *conquistadores* and the beauty of Castilian court ladies, whose blood ran in her veins. She had been accepted at Yale University Law School, and every recruiter in K Section was rubbing his hands in anticipation of adding her to the agency's select list of career officers. And then she'd slipped from their grasp.

The door opened and a waiter, perspiring in a short, white mess jacket, asked for Durell's order.

Ana interposed. "Bourbon and soda," she said.

"I'm surprised you remembered."

"I remember everything about us."

"Is that so much?"

"More than you know, dear Cajun." Her mouth arched smugly. "I have a diary full of you."

"How did you know I was in town?"

"Calvin Eisler told me. He knows about everything."

"He did?"

35

Ana nodded. Durell could not have said what she was thinking. "In fact," she said, "I am here as his emissary. He said to tell you to leave him alone." As Durell's face darkened, she added hastily, "But I knew you wouldn't. He's such an ass, really. He thinks of me as an American, although I was born in Cuba. I told him you would listen to a fellow countryman—but I just wanted an excuse to see you again." She squeezed his hand, only a bit, and said, "Do you mind?"

"He shouldn't have known my name at this point," Durell said. "He certainly should not have discussed the matter with you."

"Why not?" Her eyes went brassy. "I have an interest in this. Dick was my friend, and Calvin knows it. Dick introduced us at an embassy party, shortly after I arrived here."

Her voice held no trace of her Cuban birth and infancy. Her upbringing in the U.S. seemed to have made her totally American, Durell thought. He said, "What's Eisler to you now?"

"He wants me to marry him. I hope you're jealous."

"Why don't you?"

"I'm not ready for marriage—I want to explore life while I can, all sides of it, everything, everywhere."

"Some doors are better left closed. Remember Pandora?"

Another smile bent her small mouth. "I would have loved to be Pandora—not to loose the evils, but, once they were out anyway, to have made capital of them." She sighed, picked up her cigarette from the ashtray, saw that it had gone out and dropped it back carelessly. "Anyhow, Calvin's too unpredictable for my taste. Always popping off somewhere at odd hours, sometimes for days on end. He's something of a rebel, really."

"He's got a lot to lose, for a rebel," Durell said.

"His family's wealth is immense, if that's what you mean. But I gather that his personal share is relatively slight, what with brothers and sisters and uncles and cousins. They own several large sugar estates, timbering concessions—two or three shipping lines. His relatives

36

find him a little eccentric—they sent him to Cambridge to study the classics and mellow into a proper gentleman, but he came back with degrees in botany and tropical forestry. He's written several papers and books on the flora and fauna of Guyana. He goes into the interior frequently. But lately he's been fanatical about politics. He's impatient to make his mark—he hopes for a ministerial appointment soon."

Ana's remarks brought to Durell's mind the COMMENT section of Eisler's dossier:

> Subject volunteered collaboration in antigovernment labor agitation (1962–3) through Public Service International (U.S. cover affiliate: American Federation of State, County and Municipal Employees). Subsequent action keyed through family-dominated holdings with house unions. After fall of Marxist prime minister, was switched to political orientation with view to penetration of National Assembly. Objective accomplished, 1973. Present objective: cabinet-level post. Subject provides high-grade data on irregular basis (BUDGET subsidy: $1,200 U.S. a mo.). However, with deepening involvement, subject has displayed initiative for unauthorized pursuits on which control officer lacks information, e.g. *sub rosa* police connections, political dealing, influence peddling. Subject's tendency to self-aggrandizement and isolation from control are negative to sound operational procedures and planning. Prospects should be evaluated with care before committing present objective to budget.

It was a side to Eisler known to few persons—and no Guyanese. Chad had been right, Durell reflected. If it got out, it would shatter the man's career—and Durell did not particularly care now if that happened.

Ana was saying, "I know how you feel about what happened to Dick. I knew K Section would send someone down."

"You know nothing about K Section, Ana," Durell said.

"Would it frighten you if I did? I, who was reared among its people?"

"Their families aren't aware of that much. It's to their own benefit."

"And their foster children even less, right?"

"We did what we could for you, after your father was lost at the Bay of Pigs. He was one of the most capable of Cuban exile leaders, and we owed him that. Jim and Marge gave you a normal home; you were more than a foster child to them."

"I know, Sam. I didn't mean to sound resentful." She turned her face to the windows, where the reflected jaguars floated in savage constellation above Georgetown's trees and rooftops. There came a distant rummaging noise of wind and traffic, the spicy fragrance of Portuguese garlic pork.

Durell wondered where the waiter was and considered the Volkswagen parked below. He thought about the intentions of its occupants and whether they would be content to wait outside or come in here. If they became impatient, Ana's life could be endangered. His .38 was a comforting lump on his belt, just below his right kidney, but this room, with its globe lamps and white cedar cabinets, was a cage high in the air, a potential death trap.

Ana's eyes found his. "I want to know what you plan to do about Dick. I have a right."

"No you don't," Durell said flatly.

She took a deep breath, arrogant breasts puffing against the neckline of her dress, and crossed the long curves of her taut thighs. She looked offended, and spoke to Durell as if he were to be pitied. "You question every person, every little motive, don't you?"

"Yes."

"I wonder how I could like a man such as you. You make me so mad." She put a gold lighter to another cigarette and blew smoke at the high ceiling. "How is Deirdre?" she asked. "You haven't married her yet, have you?"

"No."

"And you never will."

"She knows that."

"Not in her heart. But that's her problem, isn't it. Do you remember that weekend on the skipjack? You thought of me as a child, but I wanted so much for you to . . . " She dropped the thought, and said, "It seems so long ago, that weekend on Chesapeake Bay."

"Only three years. It was just before you inherited your uncle's plantation and came to Guyana," Durell said. A Caribbean rhythm had begun thudding from the speaker box. The breeze stirred quiet eddies in the room, and cigarette ashes fluttered on the bottom of the ashtray.

Durell's eyes slid from Ana's beauty to the iron railing of a narrow balcony outside the room.

He wondered how one got onto it.

"I'd better go now," he said, and rose from his chair.

Her slender body moved in front of him. "Wait," she said, and slid her arms up over his shoulders. Her lips were a moist invitation; her eyes had turned to caramel. "Please don't shut me out. Dick was like an uncle to me, more than ever since I came down here. Let me help. When you are ready."

Durell regarded her eyes. She seemed able to close off her thoughts so that you could see nothing in them. He blew out a short breath. "All right," he said, "there is one thing. Go back to Eisler and try to talk him into seeing me voluntarily—I'll get to him one way or the other. Maybe you can convince him to do it the easy way."

"Of course. I'll do what I can."

The kiss she gave him was more than a quick thanks.

Durell denied the appetite it provoked and broke away. "I'll give you an hour," he said.

"That isn't very long."

"I'll be waiting at the hotel. I'll leave here first."

He opened the door and stepped onto a dusky landing at the top of the stairs and found something lying there.

It was the waiter, either dead or unconscious.

Someone was running down the stairs.

Chapter Eight

The rickety old stairs creaked and quaked as Durell bounded down, angered that Ana had spoken Calvin Eisler's name openly, angered with himself because he hadn't taken her to a more secure place when he'd realized she wanted to discuss business. The waiter had been disposed of with professional competence. There had been no sound of a struggle, no cry of pain or alarm, not even the thump of a falling body.

Whoever had been listening beyond that door knew now that Durell placed a lot of importance on a meeting with Eisler.

Which meant that Eisler's cover had been blown.

And that Eisler might not live to tell Durell anything.

Durell saw a flash of yellow, jumped the last six risers, hit the floor, taking the impact on bent knees, and angled into the bar, where an antique jukebox pumped out the clangor of a steel band recording. The bar attracted an unpretentious clientele. Fresh sputum glistened like molasses in the spittoons. They were laborers, balata bleeders, lumberjacks, prospectors in town for a day or maybe a week, a congregation that reminded you of the immense wilderness beginning some ten miles south and stretching clear across the Amazon basin to the Tropic of Capricorn.

Seen from the rear, the man Durell chased was tall, with lean hips and overdeveloped shoulders. His oily black hair was cut short above the collar of a loose-tailed yellow shirt. Then he paused just an instant to push open a rear exit and looked back, and Durell almost recoiled as the face was imprinted horribly on his memory—two pinpoints of black luminosity that were eyes in a featureless, gouty swirl of burn scars.

In back of the Toucan Patio the wind was angry and just on the cool side of tepid. The air was weighted with the reek of garbage and flowers and impending rain. Insects rattled against pumpkin-colored window panes.

Durell's dark eyes switched back and forth, his breathing light. His hand slid under his jacket and around his waist to rest on the butt of the .38 in its scabbard, and his shirt felt tight and moist beneath his armpits. The man had betrayed an overweening self-confidence up there in the wind tower, listening to the final dribble of conversation, waiting until the last moment to flee. He could be waiting to attack Durell out here in the windy gloom.

But then there came a leafy clash of branches, and Durell glimpsed the yellow shirt just as it rounded a corner to the right.

He ran hard, not knowing if the man had come here alone.

The VW still was parked where he had last seen it on the street named Orange Walk. Behind the streetlamp glaze on its windshield was the dim figure of a head. Durell started for the VW, then was aware of a slap of running feet that diminished to his left. He followed, heard the Vokswagen's engine sputter, and shook away thoughts that he had been lured into a pincers.

Near the Public Hospital two blocks away the man doubled back over a sea of mud that was crazed with plank walks and ran through a collection of stilt-supported shanties made with junk lumber and packing cases. The wet ground was checkered with light from doors and windows opened to the breeze, and Durell glimpsed people dancing inside to the tinny music of cheap radios. He smelled fried plantain *foo-foo* cakes, as he moved confidently around stilt poles and puddles, bushes and junk.

The man broke from cover near the East Coast

Railway tracks and ran past the Government Technical Institute, headed north on Camp Road.

Durell gained on him, glanced back, saw the Volkswagen puttering up the street, sinister in its lack of hurry. The wind hurled flocks of sticky pink saman blossoms like bursts of sparks.

Then Durell was on the stone rampart of the old seawall, where he saw the thin, cloud-reflected light on treacherous flats of fine mud stretched a quarter of a mile to the Atlantic, tufted with grass, heaped with seaweed. A dull, flickering belt was the ocean, dirt-brown by day with sediment from the Amazon, Oiapoque, Courantyne and countless other rivers.

The yellow shirt was a dim flag that beckoned him onward, with Georgetown to his right sprawled out on a drained marsh four feet below high tide. He tripped over necking couples, burst through knots of revelers. The smell of ozone was in the air.

A pistol made a flat sound, and people yelled and scattered. Durell threw himself prone, unlimbered his .38 S&W, fired twice, shooting high to cover himself as he rolled to the seaward lip of the wall. He hoped to catch the man from the rear.

He did not want to kill.

He wanted information.

Lightning stroked the sky, flared against human forms and white-painted gingerbread buildings down on the street. It made a bizarre moon of the blighted face that peered above an old Dutch watergate some thirty yards away.

Then a drumming torrent of rain lashed them, and Durell's eyes filled with water, his nose with mist. The cold cataract obliterated distance. Frustration roweled Durell, since he knew the man would be gone when the rainsquall had passed. He breathed a low curse and descended the seawall to the sheltered doorway of a small souvenir shop.

And there was Otelo Antunes.

The reporter stood his ground, startled black eyes

fixed on Durell. Durell normally attempted to suppress his emotions as distracting and dangerous, but he did nothing to check the surge of loathing and rage now.

He wanted to punish the man for Dick's death, maybe kill him, although logic told him that would be a gross error, and logic, detached, impersonal, refined, was what he lived by. The hatred he welcomed quickened his pulse and sharpened his eyes and made him want to do violent things with his hands. The voice of reason was faint, but he would try to listen to it. He was surprised the skinny Portuguese didn't break and run, but reporters could be arrogant behind the skirts of a press that told all.

Durell's tone was bitter, as he said: "Snooping out a story on me, Otelo?"

"You're newsworthy enough," Otelo replied.

"And that's all that counts, isn't it."

"The people have a right to know." Otelo scowled.

"Sure. Do I get killed, like Dick?"

"Maybe. I didn't ... "

Before the reporter could finish, Durell's right fist smashed into his cheek, and his body twisted from the ankles like rubber and crashed through a small display window. His knees sagged and he slid out with a debris of stuffed alligators, jam jars and seashell knickknacks. Things clinked and tinkled above the howling wind. Blood smeared the corner of Otelo's thin, loose mouth, and a red welt swelled on the side of his face. His eyes rolled, then focused on Durell towering in the blowing rain mist, fists crumpled.

Durell remembered McFee's admonition not to cause trouble with the media and suddenly concluded he did not give a damn. He spoke down at the man with solemn menace: "I want to know who leaked Dick Boyer's identity to you, and you're going to tell me, Otelo. *Now.*"

"That's privileged information," Otelo argued.

Durell reached for the man with a fury that was contemptuous and uncharacteristically careless. Too late he saw what looked to be a flashlight in a square plastic case, heard an immediate snapping report as something tapped lightly against his chest and abdomen.

All his muscles seemed to knot, and he slumped to the ground in incredible pain.

Otelo bent over him with the Taser. Now Durell recognized the unconventional weapon. Its wired darts could transmit 50,000 volts of electricity, but it was very inaccurate and could not kill. It had a range of only fifteen feet, and should have been useless against Durell, who now lay writhing on the concrete. His heartbeat was light; his head swam; punished muscles cramped his frame.

"You don't fool me, Mr. Durell," Otelo said. "You and Boyer were cut from the same bolt of cloth—and you will end as he did. We have no need of your kind in Guyana."

"You may have more need than you think," Durell panted.

Against shocked muscles, Durell attempted to lunge for Otelo. Another paralyzing current rapped through his frame. He lurched onto his side, squirming against the torment. Then it stopped, and he struggled for breath. The rain had ended; the air was soggy and cold.

"I can give you as many jolts as you ask for," Otelo said. His narrow smile glittered in the low light of the dress shop, and he spoke quickly. "It's only a matter of time before I have the facts on you."

"I'll get the name of your source out of you," Durell said with a groan. He clinched his teeth and blinked through cold sweat.

"You don't give up, do you," Otelo said. The look on Durell's face brought a hard swallow to the reporter's throat, and he added, "Well, I don't give up, either. Remember that."

He jettisoned the Taser cartridges and ran across the steamy street. His car was the Volkswagen that had followed Durell, and Durell realized why the tail had been so obvious. Otelo was just an amateur at Durell's game—but an amateur who had reminded Durell forcibly never to give way to anger; never underestimate anyone.

The Taser might just as easily have been a pistol, and Durell concluded he was lucky the lesson hadn't cost him his life.

He pushed himself to his knees, still wobbly, and his mind turned to another professional, the man with the fire-ravaged face. He wondered whose team that one played on.

The mysterious Warakabra Tiger's?

Chapter Nine

"Are you all right, sir?"

"I think so. Yes."

The policeman offered his hand and helped Durell to his feet. There were two officers, both big men with broad black faces and eyes that hid their thoughts. One had a small patch of beard in the center of his heavy chin. He made notes on damage done to the shop window. They wore short-sleeved shirts and straw hats, the wide brims tacked to one side of the crown with shining emblems. Both were armed with Webley .455 revolvers inherited from the British. They had driven up seconds after Otelo left.

"Hold onto my arm," the beardless one said.

"I can manage, thanks," Durell said. A taste of copper soured his tongue. The ocean made no sound beyond the seawall. A small cluster of people stood up there, watching. The squall had sent most home. No one was on the street.

"You look all right," the cop said. "You're a tourist? This is a bad part of town. Was anything taken from you?"

"I'm here on business. Nothing was taken."

"May I have your identification, please?"

The other officer continued to jot in his notebook, behind Durell. Durell gave the first man his papers and thought this was not going to get better; it was going to get worse. Encounters with the local police could be very sticky; he always sought to avoid them. But now he decided he'd best take the initiative. "I wish to speak with your superior," he said.

The cop's eyes could not hide a flare of surprise. Then he smiled without showing his teeth.

"Very well," he said. He handed the papers back to Durell, and the pair escorted him to their car.

Another police cruiser had arrived moments after the first. All the two cops in it had done was keep everybody at a distance from the shop. Despite the gunfire earlier and the brawl at the shop entrance, no questions were being asked of witnesses.

Maybe it was just poor procedure.

But Durell had a nagging suspicion that the police wanted him—only him—for reasons that had nothing to do with events here, and would have hauled him away in any case.

He thought he might as well ask for it.

As they drove, Durell recalled the map of Georgetown he had committed to memory, using mnemonics taught at The Farm. Police headquarters was nearby on Young Street, adjacent to the Pegasus Hotel; the Brickdam Police Station, which handled immigration and passports, was next to Saint Stanislaus College downtown.

They weren't headed toward either.

The two officers remained very polite, very courteous. They had not troubled to search him, and he still had his .38 and could have blown their heads off where they sat in front of him, beyond a wire screen.

He was sure now that this had all been prearranged; that the police had been looking for him, possibly for several hours.

He glanced backward. No one seemed to be following them. The teeming stars hung in a bright sky that was free of clouds for the moment. He sat back and noted the landmarks along their route and considered what to do with the big diamond.

He had gone out of his way to make the stone obvious at the hotel desk. It was too soon to know if anyone had taken the bait.

With the world diamond supply monopolized by the Central Selling Organization in London, there would always be smuggling, and the big diamond hinted at some kind of illicit Guyanese operation. But the submarine on the river had been ample evidence of something infinitely more menacing than diamond smuggling.

Durell surmised that Dick had been killed because he knew what it was.

He disregarded the news story that blew Dick's cover as a clever ploy to misdirect investigation of the murder. If Dick had been hiding, or on the run, the two-day lag between publication and Dick's death would have been an acceptable risk for his assassins, just so long as Dick never managed to communicate his intelligence to anyone else.

The police radio made throat-clearing sounds as the car bumped across a railroad siding and stopped before a steel warehouse, its high facade a sheet of black shadow. Durell saw dock cranes against the luminous sky. Ship funnels glowed beyond the warehouse roof. He was escorted from the car and scented bilge oil and garbage from below, where the river purled among pier supports. Ship's machinery and dock equipment clattered and hummed and screeched.

The warehouse was redolent of coffee and fruits inside, the air still and humid.

Durell was shown into a suite of offices, utilitarian, sparsely furnished with steel desks and chairs. Shipping schedules were on the walls, bills of lading, invoices, ledgers on the desks.

The beardless policeman spoke quietly. "Please wait here, sir," he said, and went through a door. Durell could not see in there.

The big policeman with the toy beard was a black tower beside him. Sweat shone on the man's forehead, ran down his cheeks. His Webley was still in its holster, almost as if tempting Durell to try for it.

The other cop reappeared, motioned Durell inside.

The man awaiting him there was squat. He had a rigid Prussian neck, the hardened features of a drill sergeant. The hand he offered was a mahogany plank.

"I am Inspector Sydney James, Guyana National Police. Your safety here is my personal responsibility."

"That explains it, then."

"The civilities? Do not regard them too highly."

"I don't."

James eyed him severely. His eyes were a beautiful brown, the color of coffee beans. He bent an arm and scooped his hand toward a steel chair. "Sit down," he said. The inspector saw a strand of lint on his jacket sleeve, grimaced, flicked it away. He wore an expensive navy-blue suit that should have been beyond his means. A large diamond ring graced the little finger of his left hand.

Durell took the chair, crossed his legs widely, and said: "Something else needs explaining, doesn't it?"

"You have a question?"

"Why the warehouse? Surely you have a normal office."

James cleared his throat with a small grunt. "I'm a busy man. Constantly on the move, you see. This location happens to be convenient for me at the moment."

"And keeps our little *tête-à-tête* off the record?"

"Don't be presumptuous, Mr. Durell." James' gaze turned cool as the rain that had fallen. "Where did you find the diamond?"

"So. You're interested in the diamond. Another explanation," Durell said. "I see now why you had me brought here."

"Just answer my question."

"Maybe I found it lying on the ground."

Durell was startled when the inspector laughed. His teeth were as pretty as his eyes. Then James said, "I expected evasion. It does not trouble me; it makes my point."

"Which is?"

"You have no prospecting permit and no bill of sale. You have nothing to prove that you have legal possession of the diamond."

"How do you know I have no bill of sale?"

"Do you?"

Durell was silent. There was a snapping sound as an electric wall clock moved its minute hand.

The inspector sighed theatrically. "I'm afraid you are in violation of our laws, Mr. Durell. You will be sent back to the U.S.A. first thing in the morning."

Durell was fairly certain that Eisler had put James up to this, as he remembered the mention of "*sub rosa* police connections" in Eisler's dossier. But he judged he would gain nothing by throwing such an accusation in the inspector's self-satisfied face, and, looking at the two cops standing by the door, he could end the worse for it.

The inspector was speaking, his voice heavy with emphasis. "Do I make myself clear, Mr. Durell? First thing in the morning, or you will be arrested, charged with illegal possession and smuggling, and held in confinement, pending the outcome of your trial. It could take weeks—or months."

"You haven't got a case, inspector."

James made another offhand gesture. "Oh? That would not come out until the trial was held."

Durell drew a long breath. "All right, inspector. You win. I have just one other question."

"You may ask it."

"You could have told me all of this in your office at police headquarters. So what did you really bring me here for?"

James' eyes snapped, and his heavy shoulders drew up, and he did not look like a Prussian, or a banker, which he vaguely resembled in more relaxed moments, or anything, except a mad cop. His voice was tightly controlled, as he said: "What they say about you is true, Mr. Durell. You are a clever man."

Then he whirled a finger at his two men and pointed at the door, and they went out, and he followed.

The door closed, and Durell was left to sit and wonder.

Durell could not figure it out at first. He checked the door and found it unlocked and looked into the great dusky barn of the warehouse. No one was there. He was aware of a sense of entrapment, although he knew with certainty that the outer door of the warehouse would be unlocked also. The incessant tradewind moaned against the enormous tin roof, and he felt something like hackles begin to rise at the back of his neck. He stood on the threshold of the office and his face turned from the warehouse to the office and back. He heard a scrape as the door to the street, beyond high-piled hemp bags of copra, was swung open. He slid back into the office and closed the door.

It could be employees of the warehouse firm, or it could be a nightwatchman.

He did not think it was either.

He pressed an ear against the door and heard the muffled footfalls of someone approaching. There appeared to be no other exit, and the frugal, barren space of the office made it pointless to hide. He moved to the center of the room and waited, poised, he hoped, for whatever might come. At least he could be thankful that Inspector James had left him his gun.

Then the door to the office opened.

The face of a small Chinese that peered at him did not appear even remotely surprised. Durell remembered the Chinese-made pistol, the Tokarev, that Peta had carried, and his face hardened as his fingers moved backward along his belt, ready for the draw of his .38.

The face disappeared. Something was said in Mandarin of the northern variety, in which Durell was fluent, but he could not hear well enough to interpret it. Then a different face came into view; the door swung wider as only the second man entered, then closed behind him.

And Durell figured it out.

"Stay where you are, Colonel Su," he said. He did not quite have his hand on the grip of his pistol.

"Of course, Mr. Durell. But you have nothing to

fear from me, for the moment." He was a big, bulky Manchurian with a nose that was no more than a low bas-relief on his flat face. His eyes were alert, intelligent slits of black liquid. His mouth showed a ruthless competence and control. The humidity made quills of his short, salt-and-pepper hair, and he looked almost shabby in a poorly tailored gray business suit.

"How much did you pay James to set this up?" Durell asked.

"You jump to conclusions. A trait of your race, I fear."

Durell wondered where the other man was—how *many* others there might be. "I'm to believe this is just a coincidence? That Colonel Su Chung, Black House, Lotus Section stumbled into me in a warehouse?" Durell did not take his hand from his belt.

"You know me?"

"I know you. So do people all over Southeast Asia, not a few of them dead now."

Su shrugged his shoulders. "Times have changed. As for this James you mention, I know of him only distantly. This warehouse is leased to us; those commodities out there are for shipment to the People's Republic of China. One of our men found you here. What was he to do but call his security officer?" Su smiled. It was a small wink of teeth, then gone.

"Very well," Durell said. "James is covered. And now . . . ?"

"Now that I see the interloper is no common burglar, but Samuel Cullen Durell, chief field agent for the infamous K Section of the CIA, it happens that I have something to discuss with him."

The teeth winked at Durell again. He decided one was gold, but it was hard to tell. Durell thought of the other man—or men—again. "Am I free to leave here?" he tested.

Su nodded. "Whenever you wish, but . . . "

"No buts." Durell jerked open the office door and strode through the gloom of the storage area. No one was about. He did not look back. He went through the warehouse door, showing himself in the street, and studied the parking area. A Mercedes with a diplomatic license plate was parked there, about twenty-five yards away. He could not say how many men were inside it, but none of them got out to challenge him. He counted a few seconds, and, when there still was no reaction, he went back inside.

Su had not moved. He began talking the moment Durell returned, his husky voice thoughtful, almost professorial. "As you may know," he said, "the People's Republic of China has lent friendly assistance to the people of Guyana in constructing a dam on a tributary of the Mazaruni River, not far from Tumereng." He paused, lifted thin brows toward Durell.

"Go on."

"At about 2000 hours, local time, on the night of the third, a man known to us in Southeast Asia as William Bryce Haddenfield—and here as Richard Boyer, your so-called brother-in-law—was apprehended by us at the construction site of that dam."

The third, Durell recalled, was the night of Boyer's desperate transmission to K Section headquarters.

Colonel Su continued: "I know it would be wasting my time to ask you what Boyer was doing there—one does not attempt to draw nectar from a thorn. We have drawn our own conclusions. Mr. Boyer was questioned in vain, then placed under guard for removal to Guyanese authorities. To our embarrassment, he overwhelmed our man, injuring him slightly, and escaped. Needless to say, security has been strengthened now."

Durell's mind turned back through the files he had read in Dick's office and came up blank. There was no mention of the dam among his papers. Everything must have come down on Dick's head at once, Durell thought, sending him deep into the rain forest, to the dam. To his death. He raised dark eyes to Colonel Su, and said, "If you have a protest, take it to the ambassador."

"No, Mr. Durell. You are chief field agent for K Section. My words are heard where they count most, without any diplomatic obfuscation." Su's voice became angry, eyes squeezed to two inky lines. "The dam is our first major effort in the Western Hemisphere to show underdeveloped countries what the people's revolution can do for them. We will not have that endangered by agents of the United States. Be forewarned. Diplomatically, doors have been opened between our countries. They can be closed." He paused, and added, "And between men such as you and me, who remember the old days—well, I would welcome the excuse to settle some accounts."

"I'd be happy to accommodate you, but I have other orders," Durrell replied. "Besides, the inspector says he's sending me home tomorrow."

"I'm not stupid; you will leave when you are ready."

The two men stared at each other, and Durell said, "I don't know why Dick should have been on your property. Your story could be pure fantasy, dreamed up after the fact. How can I know that you didn't kill our man?"

The teeth winked again. Durell thought the big Manchurian had the meanest grin he had ever seen.

Colonel Su said, "You cannot know, given the fact that neither of us trusts the other in the slightest degree." And then he added: "Just stay away from the dam."

Durell picked up his rental Fiat at the Toucan Patio, urgently aware that time was an angry tide threatening to sweep him away. Somewhere, Durell told himself, Dick had left a trail that would lead him through the riddle of the submarine and the Warakabra Tiger itself.

But by morning Durell would be a fugitive, Georgetown untenable for all practical purposes, and the jungle, without a clear path and focused destination, simply a place to die in slow agony.

His best hope was Calvin Eisler.

And he was to the point where he would use any means to extract information from the unwilling man.

Chapter Ten

Durell switched on the light in his hotel room, methodically checked closet and bathroom. No one had been there. His watch read 12:47. Thanks to Inspector James and Colonel Su he had missed his assigned transmission frame. He would just have to intrude on another station's time, he decided.

Breaking open his suitcase, he withdrew an ordinary-looking 60-watt lightbulb that was packed in a retail box of blue and white cardboard, and a small package of expensive stationery and a pair of reading glasses in a lightweight frame of dark plastic.

He screwed the lightbulb into the bedside lamp, slipped on the glasses and opened the stationery. The first two pages contained a letter to Dick's sister that Durell had begun while on the jet to Guyana. It spoke prosaically of the flight, remorse over the loss of Durell's "brother-in-law" and hopes of a quick return to his "wife." He put the last page of the letter on the table beside the lamp, as if in the act of completing the correspondence, then held the inner surface of the top of the stationery box under the light.

The chemical coating inside the bulb combined with the polarized eyeglasses to bring out a dense listing of code words and phrases in the box top.

Durell made no notes, memorizing the encoded message as he composed it. Then he pressed a rivet on the hinge of his suitcase, releasing its plastic shell liner, and took out a small microphone.

The powerful signal of the JCT-Mk9 transceiver spanned 2,000 nautical miles to the sealed, fluorescent-lighted guts of K Section.

"Kappa Sigma, Kappa Sigma. Tiger requests intrude."

There was a silence. Then, "Read you, Tiger. Hold."

Another pause, longer this time. Durell's eyes wandered to the door, then past a factory reproduction of a neo-African wood carving that hung above the fruitwood bedstead, and he stared through the slats of the Demerara window, seeing nothing.

"Mocha says negative, Tiger."

"Read Tiger's request as a Q pre-empt," Durell asserted.

Mocha was Columbia Control. That would be Barry Symonds, a young hound on his way up, jealous of his operation, tenacious of his every prerogative, but a good man. Durell was taking a chance that Mocha's was a routine report. The sweephand of his watch moved through the space of fifteen seconds, then thirty. He resisted the impulse to switch frequencies and listen to Barry bitch.

Finally headquarters spoke: "You're cleared to proceed, Tiger."

Durell spoke slowly and distinctly, giving equal emphasis to each word. "Mangos steady. Bacon up. Eight-two and three-four. Ten hundred hours Demerara in. Plentiful coconuts. Turkeys and sugar in demand. Five-seven and eight-six. Turtles. One shipment. Unknown quality. Ten hundred hours Demerara out. Southern Cross brand strong. Coconuts down. Oranges available. Seventeen-four and nine-eight. Limes steady . . . "

Durell continued the random numbers and commodities for another ten seconds, but the communications specialist at the other end of the transmission no longer listened or cared. Only that portion of the message between the mentions of coconuts had counted. The rest was merely to obscure and confuse unauthorized ears.

Durell hoped the ASW T-3A Orions out of Guantánamo Bay were lucky enough to get a fix on the sub and identify its nationality, but the block of ocean contained within his coordinates was large, and he doubted any success.

"Southern Cross brand" had tagged the search with

urgent priority and asked for a report at Durell's next time window.

As he unscrewed the lightbulb, his telephone rang.

He ignored it, carefully replaced the microphone, bulb, stationery and reading glasses in the suitcase. When he was satisfied, he picked up the receiver.

"Sam?" The voice was Ana's.

"Did you speak with Eisler?"

"Yes, but—"

"What did he say?"

"He said to stay away. He was angry with me for even asking."

Durell said nothing.

"Sam—what happened when you left the Toucan Patio? I heard you run down the stairs. I couldn't catch up."

"Someone eavesdropped on us. He got away."

It was Ana's turn to be silent. Then she said: "They know I'm trying to help you?"

"Maybe. Don't be frightened."

"You might as well make it official."

"What?"

"That I'm working for you. I don't mean really official, of course. Just between us."

"No," Durell said.

"You got me into this."

"You got yourself in, Ana."

"I'm coming up, Sam. I'm staying with you."

"Ana ... !" Durell wiped his brow, weighed alternatives. "Are you in the lobby?" he said.

"Yes."

"And you still want to stick your neck out?"

"I'll do anything you ask, Sam."

"Take the elevator to the second floor. I'll meet you there."

No one moved in the second-floor corridor at this time of night. No one made a sound that Durell could hear, where he stood in the entrance to the back stairs and watched the elevator doors. When Ana stepped out, long-legged, face golden and eyes glowing with excitement in the low light, Durell beckoned from the stairs. She hurried to him, and he turned his back and started down. A moment later, he heard her close behind.

"Where are you taking me?" she asked.

"There's somewhere I want to go, and *you're* going to take *me*."

It was only two blocks from the Berbice Hotel to the ferry stelling and Stabroek Market, which kept the former Dutch name of the town. Beneath its red-capped clock tower and cast-iron roof were hundreds of shops patronized by thousands of people a day. You could buy almost anything there, from straw hats and native diamonds cut by imported Hollanders to Amerindian baskets and *diyas,* small earthen lamps used in celebration of *Deepavali,* the Hindu festival of lights.

Durell and Ana were on foot. They appeared to be free of surveillance.

"This way," Ana said, and they turned left, keeping to the star shade across from the market's macadam parking lot. A row of yellow public transit buses had been stored there for the night, otherwise it was empty. The wind hummed in the telephone wires.

Durell kept Ana moving at a normal pace, judging that a strolling couple aroused little suspicion and hoping that Ana's company would throw off-balance anyone who might be on the alert for him alone.

Half a block northward they came to a long arcade beneath a balcony that was screened-in and roofed with slanting metal sheets.

"It's in there," Ana said.

"Come on," Durell replied.

Even this far away Stabroek Market smelled of molasses, squashed oranges, poultry. The chuffing of a switching engine came from the docks a few hundred yards away. As they entered the arcade, passing beneath a big breadfruit tree, something thrashed above them, a coati, perhaps, or a kinkajou after birds.

Durell counted the shops they strolled past.

"That's the one," Ana said. She nodded toward the fourth door. "Guyana Exports. Aquarium Fish. Supplies," a sign over the door read.

They went between buildings, treading through rank grass and cricket sounds, then felt their way along the dark rear wall. Durell glanced back. Ana's face was hidden in the night. He did not know her thoughts, but she did not act afraid. He counted the doors. A white van was parked at the fourth one, the one that would lead into the rear area of Calvin Eisler's shop.

The van was locked, so Durell shone his pencil flash through the rear window, into the cargo compartment, and saw a couple of empty plastic buckets, a scooplike net. He looked through the driver's window and saw, between the seats, a neat bundle of shipping tags imprinted with "Air Freight" and "Timehri International Airport."

When he turned around, Ana was smoking one of her silver-tipped cigarettes. Durell snatched it and ground it into the earth. She drew back a step. "I just wanted something to calm my nerves," she said.

"Have you ever been in here?" he asked, as he hefted a heavy padlock on the shop's rear door. He withdrew a leather case from his inside jacket pocket.

"I didn't know you were going to break into the place."

"Does that bother you?"

"Not particularly. You didn't have to snatch my cigarette away."

Durell examined the picks in the leather case and chose one under the brief flare of his pen flash. "Answer my question," he said, bending to the lock.

"Yes, I've been in there. It's just a shop."

"Layout?"

"Large storage room in the rear. The rest is retail space, except for a counter at the front."

A few twists of the pick and the lock sprung loose. Durell put his hand across the small of Ana's back, urging her inside, cast his eyes briefly up and down the alley, then followed her and closed the door.

They groped through an unlighted storage area into the main space of the shop, and Durell let out a slow breath. There were scores of aquariums, large and small. A few were illuminated, the only source of light here. They contained a dazzling variety of tropical fish, many indigenous to Guyana: glowlight tetras, beacon fish, four-eyes, leaf fish, hatchet fish. Their glass-walled habitats were stacked against walls, on tables, on the floor. The room had a fresh, watery scent, and aerators gurgled, tiny pumps whizzed.

On one side of the room was a large tank that contained a score or more of piranhas. Durell thought of the dead frogman. "Popular item?" he asked.

"Not ordinarily," Ana said. "They are for sale more as curiosities than anything." She followed his eyes to a plank table beside the tank. It held a bloody aluminum tray and a small pile of broom straws. "Sometimes he allows people the fun of feeding them," she said. "You stick a piece of liver on the end of a straw and dip it into the tank, and *zip!*—all you draw out is half a straw." Her small mouth smiled at him.

"Where's the phone?"

She pointed. "Over there, behind the counter."

Durell stepped behind the old brass cash register, racks of pamphlets, fish food. He could see onto the street from a window here, and he kept to the shadows, watching outside, as the other end of the line made a burring sound. When an answer came, he said: "May I speak with Mr. Eisler, please?"

There was only distant courtesy in the reply: "Mr. Eisler is not taking calls. Mr. Eisler has retired."

"Tell him I'm calling on behalf of Inspector James."

A clanking sound came over the line as the phone was laid on a table. Durell's gaze roamed over the twisting fish, the attentive oval of Ana's face, then back outside. His eyes were dark and brooding in his sun-browned face.

"Calvin Eisler speaking."

"This is Sam Durell."

"Oh. Please hang up and go back into the woodwork." The line did not go dead.

"I'm at your shop. Meet me here in fifteen minutes," Durell said.

"Preposterous! I'll have you arrested."

"Ana's here. They'll have to arrest her, too."

Eisler's voice, with a notable pretension to a British accent, was condescending. "I believe I can obtain her release without difficulty," he said. Then, with ominous gravity: "But I most certainly will press charges against you."

"I don't think so. I'll clarify for you, Cal. We've already been bruised down here. Pretty badly. Our image is shot anyhow, for the time being. It won't harm us that much more if we lose you, too."

There was a hesitation. Then Eisler said, "Is that some kind of threat?"

"Just the opposite. The other side knows I want to talk with you—one of them overheard Ana and me discussing it tonight. We can give you sanctuary in our embassy until this matter is concluded. No one need know you were ever there. Of course, the offer stands only if you cooperate—otherwise, they can have you."

Eisler's voice was a sneer. "I don't need your protection, Durell."

"You will—after I give Dick's file on you to Otelo Antunes."

"You—you wouldn't."

"Just expediency, Cal. I've tried to be nice."

The aquariums bubbled and fizzed. Ana stood close, and Durell's nostrils detected the fragrance of her imported perfume.

"Fifteen minutes?" Eisler said.

"Sooner, if possible."

"Don't let anybody see you in my shop, you bastard."

Durell hung up, rolled his lips under, looked out the window, then back at Ana. She gave him a thin smile and moved the supple length of her body around the counter and sat down on a wooden stool next to him.

"Nothing to do now but wait," Durell said.

They waited.

Chapter Eleven

The leaves of the breadfruit, flat black cutouts against the night, danced with sudden snips of light, and Durell saw a Jaguar sedan ease around a corner and roll into the parking area in front of the shop. The headlamps did not go out when it stopped.

"That's his car," Ana said.

"Stay out of the light," Durell said.

Tension coiled tighter as the seconds stretched out. Durell kept his face out of sight. The headlamps dazzled through the window with a fluttering of thin, gray insect shadows.

Ana spoke impatiently. "Why doesn't he come in?"

Durell shook his head.

She reached for the door.

"Stay back," he commanded, his fingers squeezed around her upper arm.

"Durell? We'll talk in my car." The voice from beyond the door was blandly pleasing, slightly British.

Durell cut his eyes to Ana.

"It really is Calvin," she said.

"Let him come to us—don't give him an advantage," Durell said.

The headlamps made vision to the outside impossible; they wove veils of reflection and counterreflection back and forth across the room. Motes of dust sparkled in the air. The idling of the Jaguar's engine was a dimly heard thrumming.

"Durell! Come, now. Really."

There was a low muttering of voices.

"How many do you judge he has with him?" Durell asked quietly.

"A chauffeur; two, maybe three bodyguards. They often accompany him."

Durell remained flattened against the wall, smelling the dankness from within it, the varnish of its veneer paneling. "Check the alley. Don't be obvious about it," he said.

As Ana walked to the back of the shop, he yelled: "Come in here, Eisler. Just you."

"What's the matter? Don't you trust me?"

Durell thought he heard low, sinister laughter. Maybe Eisler just liked to have muscle around him—but there was the possibility that he intended harm. Durell did not even consider the idea of meeting him among his men.

Ana came back through the shimmering dusk, hair afire with reflected radiance of the headlamps, some strain evident now in the forward thrust of shoulders and head. She said, "A car just turned into the alley. I closed the door."

"Good girl. The damned thing can't be locked from the inside, can it?"

"Nope." Her mouth showed a helpless grin.

Durell began sweating.

It was clear now that the lengthening silence indicated a waiting game, while some of Eisler's men tried to take them from the rear. He moved away from the window and told Ana: "Call me if they try to force the front door."

"Yo, Cajun," she said.

He smiled at her unaccustomed use of a word common to the vocabulary of K Section men. It jarred against her sleek and pampered appearance.

Her eyes read his, and she said: "I could have been as good at this as you, you know. Sometimes I wish I'd tried it."

He moved rapidly into the further dimness, through the blubbering of aquariums, until he was in the storeroom. To the untrained eye, it was a black void, formless and featureless. He watched the rear wall from the sides of his pupils, calculated his distance from the door, balanced his stance. His ears picked up the scuffing of shoes on gravel.

Then the door opened a cautious inch, three inches, eight . . .

The sky was a silver lamé of stars seen through the crack. A cool breath of air crept inside with the murmur of distant traffic, the slumberous sighing of the city. There was no sound of voices.

A heavy man entered sideways, an arm stretched out before him, a liquid gleam of metal at its end.

Durell held back until the man's shoulders pressed fully through the threshold, then he yanked him off balance, threw a savage chop at the back of his neck. The man's knees drove into the floor, and he crashed headlong onto his face. Durell swept up the fallen pistol, a Browning semiautomatic to judge by the heft and feel of it, and concentrated on the slab of glowing night that was the crack of the doorway.

"Jimmy?"

The voice was bewildered, neither alarmed nor angry yet.

"You fall over something, man?"

Durell wondered how many were out there. It hardly mattered. There was no turning back. Thoughts of Ana, alone at the front of the store, and of Eisler, waiting outside, crossed his mind.

A large, round darkness came into view. It wore a straw hat. The whisper was harsh: "Hey! Jimmy!"

As Durell watched, the hat moved forward, the eyes beneath its brim unseeing in here.

Abruptly there came a hissing intake of breath, and the hat swiveled urgently from side to side. The man had stumbled over his pal, and his weapon was swinging up blindly. Durell's Browning crunched against his head. There was a ripe *thunk!* and a grunt of pain as the man's hat and pistol went spinning away. This one had an iron skull. He bulled into the darkness, massive arms groping for his tormentor. A bucket-sized hand raked across Durell's chest, and Durell slid smoothly aside as the man bellowed and grabbed again.

This time Durell swung harder, felt the impact of steel

63

against bone up to his elbows. The man's eyes rolled white, and he reeled into a stand of shelves and pulled them down on top of him with the clatter of a rock slide.

Surprise was a thing of the past, as Durell leveled the heavy Browning at the door, his breathing light, his ears sharp.

He counted slowly. Ten came and went, then twenty. He leaned carefully to the opening.

A Ford shone coldly in the starshine. No one else was out there. He was free to take Ana and run for it, but that would not get him Eisler. He stared at the weapon in his hand, his sense of frustration mounting.

Abruptly he raised the gun and fired three rapid shots at the stars.

Someone yelled from the living space above the shops. Durell ran back to Ana, found her standing stiffly, hands clamped together, eyes wide. He grabbed her arm, pushed her toward the front door.

"The shots . . . ?" she said.

"A diversion."

He unlocked the latch, darted the width of the sidewalk through a blaze of headlamps. As he had expected, the men who were with Eisler here had run to the back alley. Eisler stood alone, and Durell threw him roughly against the side of the Jaguar and ground the Browning's muzzle into the tall, slender man's muscular belly.

"Don't . . . !" Eisler averted his aristocratic face, crossed his hands.

"Get in the car; fasten the seat belt and shoulder harness and keep your hands on the dash." He shoved the man inside and slipped under the wheel. As Ana jumped in a rear door, he threw the short floor shift into reverse. They hurtled back, stopped, the engine gunned and they lurched into the street on screaming tires.

Eisler's flesh was pasty under his suntan. His jaw muscles trembled. His face was lean and clean of form, molded around a prominent, angular nose. His eyes were blue and critical above a stubborn mouth. For all his lineage and superficial culture, he looked as dangerous and unforgiving as the jungle that had filled and hardened his physique. He wore a watery green shirt-jac of silk and immaculate white trousers.

Durell cut his eyes across the rearview mirror, saw the Ford spin away from the shop in pursuit. The men decoyed to the alley had wasted no time in recovering. Then the mirror showed Ana's eyes, expectant, surprisingly amused. She was having a good time.

Eisler swallowed heavily, and said: "If you've killed anybody . . . "

"Just knots and bruises." Durell laid the Browning in his lap and whipped the car around a turn, its tires wailing, then slowed to within the speed limit. He didn't want to attract the police. "You shouldn't have brought those goons with you," he said.

"I have a right to that file you mentioned. I brought them with me to make sure I got it."

"You didn't think I had it with me, did you?"

"You'd have been happy enough to retrieve it, wherever it is, after my men finished with you."

"You have a very poor attitude for a paid agent, Cal." Eisler snorted and crossed his arms and sulked.

"Put your hands back on the dash," Durell said in a low, even voice.

Eisler leaned against the dash. "What's Ana doing here?" he demanded.

"I made her come."

Eisler twisted his head toward Ana. "Has he harmed you?"

"He wouldn't do that, would you, Sam?"

Durell said: "Tell me what Dick was onto when he was killed."

Eisler's chuckle was grim. "What makes you think I would know?"

"According to his station log, you were the last man he talked with in Georgetown."

"So?"

"The topic was the Warakabra Tiger," Durell said.

"There is no Warakabra Tiger," Ana said. "There have

been tales of such animals since the first explorers—it's just another abominable snowman, a superstition."

"Maybe," Durell agreed. "Dick thought it might be otherwise. He asked Eisler to check on it, but there is no log entry to show that his instructions were carried out."

"Then he neglected to make one," Eisler said. "Perhaps he was in a hurry to go see for himself."

"See what?" Durell said.

Eisler ran fingers through his limp, blond hair. They were passing the Botanic Gardens now, and on one corner was the enormous wooden residence of the prime minister. It had a multicolored awning above the main entrance and a tin roof. The Ford was still behind them, not too close, and Durell judged that Eisler's men had chosen against a high-speed chase for fear of harming their boss. He continued to loaf the Jaguar along, confident and at ease in the deep, leather bucket seat, no destination in mind, the Browning solid reassurance against his thigh.

"According to my information, porkknockers—prospectors, that is—have been deserting their diggings like the devil himself was out there," Eisler said. "Some of them have been killed, mutilated. They say the Tiger makes a sound that chills the blood."

"Men have been killed? What about the police?"

"There's no police presence in that wilderness. It's dog eat dog."

Durell's voice was grim: "Then if someone manages to scare the others out, he's got it all to himself."

"That would be very difficult to do," Eisler said.

"But not impossible. Where did you get your information?"

"When Boyer asked my help, I told one of my employees, Peta Gibaudan, to inquire about it on his next buying trip into the interior."

"Peta is employed by you?" Durell asked.

"Peta is totally uncivilized," Ana said. "I doubt that you could believe anything he said. He lives near me—when he isn't roaming the forests like an animal."

"He's good at what he does, Ana," Eisler countered. "He goes deep into the interior to contact Indians who

66

catch rare fish. He arranges their transportation to Bartica, where I pick the fish up by air. I liked him well enough to grubstake his father." Eisler turned from Ana to Durell. "Claudius is an untrustworthy old porkknocker—an ex-convict from Devil's Island in French Guiana. He let Indians raise the boy, while he went off and mucked around in the woods."

"So Peta's father is a prospector," Durell mused. Some things were beginning to fall into place. "A diamond prospector?" he asked.

"I'm sure diamonds would do," Eisler said. "Of course, there's gold as well."

"And where, in Guyana's seventy thousand square miles of rain forest, is the Warakabra Tiger supposed to have its lair?"

Eisler kept just the tips of his fingers on the dash as he leaned back a bit and tried to make himself more comfortable. The Jaguar murmured, hardly audible. "Well," Eisler said, "nobody knows the exact location, of course—nobody who has lived to tell. But it's somewhere in the Mazaruni-Potaro District."

Durell's fingers tightened on the steering wheel. He told himself he should have known: the Warakabra Tiger and the Chinese dam were in the same district—and maybe the two locations were one and the same.

Maybe the Chinese were behind the Warakabra Tiger. Maybe they had something hidden at the dam and had killed Dick because he'd found it.

But what could it be? he asked himself in bewilderment. The dam would become public property day after tomorrow; the dedication ceremony with all the bigwigs had already been scheduled.

All Durell knew was that he, too, must go there.

And that Su would be waiting.

Chapter Twelve

Durell had driven into the confusion of tiny shanties that was Tiger Town, the city's worst slum. Harlots in orchid-colored dresses and drunks roamed the streets or leaned sullenly in doorways; predatory packs of youths out of work, hopeless of finding it, prowled among the unpainted houses. The air smelled of open latrines, chicken and goat droppings, soursoup tea and pigtail stew. The ceaseless wind combed trees and bushes in postage stamp gardens, where charms called *gobis* were buried to protect the plants. Beside the road, peeping frogs chirped from marshy grass.

Eisler did not care for the place at all.

"What are we doing here?" he said.

"Just driving," Durell replied.

A wheedling tone came into Eisler's voice. "You—you're not going to—to reveal my past associations, are you? You won't give my file to Otelo? I've cooperated."

"At gunpoint," Durell rasped.

"But—listen. I've had your best interests at heart. If you get as deeply involved as Boyer was, the same thing will happen to you. You should return to the U.S. Give the East Indians time to cool off." Eisler's voice was earnest as he added, "Publication of Dick's status with K Section must have been a terrible shock to them—highly inflammatory. He had begun meddling among them, apparently trying to win their confidence for some reason. I hope it was to keep a step ahead of a Marxist recrudescence, but who knows? I had word that he'd attended some of their bottom-house meetings—they call them that, because they are held secretly among the stilts beneath their houses. They aren't very happy with the situation here, because they have a racial majority, but the party of the minority blacks has managed to retain power since the turmoil of the sixties. Boyer owned a small house in Bartica, sealed since his death by the police, and may have used it for similar meetings—"

Durell cut him off: "Did you say Dick owned a house in Bartica?"

Eisler stared at him, blue eyes surprised. "Yes. Have I been helpful?"

"Yes. Maybe."

"About that file . . ." Eisler ventured.

Durell lifted the Browning and pointed its 9mm muzzle at Eisler's face. Eisler's cheeks went hollow. Durell said: "Take off your seat belt and shoulder harness. Easy does it."

Eisler handled the restraints as if they were made of pastry.

Durell said: "When I stop the car, Cal, you will run out there through those shanties. I'll be watching with this—" he hefted the Browning "—until you are out of sight. So don't stop."

Eisler suddenly found his indignation. "You're not going to put me out here?"

"This is as good a place as any, Cal." Durell's voice was bland.

"What about Ana?"

"You wouldn't want me to leave her in this slum, would you?"

Eisler's face hardened, and his eyes flashed and flickered like a rainy season squall. "You haven't heard the last of this," he hissed. He pronounced "last" like "lost."

The Jaguar scrunched to a halt, and Durell told him: "Open your door and run like hell."

Aware of the pistol in Durell's grip, Eisler did just that. Durell watched the few seconds it took for the shining white slacks to be swallowed up in the dirty shadows. Then, just as the following car was slowing to his bumper, he jammed the accelerator to the floor.

By the time the men back there found Eisler and got back to their car, he and Ana were blocks away.

At the hotel, Durell sent Ana on to his room, while he stopped at the desk to retrieve the big diamond. He rang the bell. There still was some activity here in the lobby, mostly comings and goings at the bamboo-grilled bar that opened off to one side. Durell rang the bell again, twice. A fat man ambled into view, double chins quivering, marble-sized nose held high. Durell requested his package from the safe.

The man said Durell had no package in the safe.

"I left it here, earlier in the evening," Durell said.

"Of course you did. I know you did," said the Portugese. He lifted his hands and let them fall to his sides, as he said, "But the police took it."

Durell stared evenly at him. "When?"

"Oh—over an hour ago. Two hours? You see, they demanded it. I gave it to them." He shrugged his shoulders, and his chins spilled down over the knot of his necktie. "Alas," he said.

"Alas," Durell said. He strode rapidly for the elevator.

It made sense; Inspector James must have had the diamond even as they talked in the warehouse. The diamond was the only evidence that could put Durell safely and more or less legally out of circulation. James would have been too clever to leave it at the hotel, where Durell might take it and run.

Then Durell had another thought and wished he hadn't had to come back to the Berbice at all.

Eisler would most likely call James. There would be cries of assault, kidnaping, car theft—he didn't trouble to list more.

And now he might expect the police at any moment.

Durell's mind rode above alarmed instincts to consider the problem clearly and efficiently, as he left the elevator and turned down the hall toward his room.

He still had Eisler's file, and there was no doubt that the national assemblyman regarded its release to the press with a mortal fear. But that game could be played two ways. If Eisler got Durell put away incommunicado, even for twenty-four hours, he could arrange to blow Durell's cover in the press—and when Durell obtained his release, no one would believe that what he revealed about Eisler was anything more than vengeful fabrication. And, Durell's usefulness on this mission would be at an end.

Point, counterpoint. Move, countermove.

Maybe Eisler wouldn't take the risk. But he was hurt, furious, unforgiving, and maybe he would.

Meanwhile, some alien force was eating into this little country like cancer, perhaps to spread all through South America.

Durell burst impatiently into his room, slammed the door behind him, heaved his suitcase onto the bed and began packing. The splatter of the shower came to his ears, and he looked around and saw Ana's black dress, draped carelessly over the back of a chair, her slippers beside it.

Someone rapped on the door.

Durell's hands hesitated over the suitcase.

The knocking came again, louder this time.

He dropped the heavy Browning into the suitcase, snapped the luggage closed, slid it under the bed. He took the snub-nosed .38 S&W—his favorite weapon—from its holster and held it in loose fingers as he leaned his ear against the door. If it were the police, he'd have to take them. He did not think that would be too difficult, judging by the cops he'd seen so far. He could not allow them to destroy his mission. He reached out, flicked off the lights.

He heard nothing; he said nothing. The knock did not sound again. The shower rumbled.

Then came the pad of foottreads, moving away.

He let out his breath, turned on the lights, and heard a voice at his back:

"Don't move. Drop your gun first."

Durell remembered with regret that, in his haste to pack, he had not checked the window that opened onto the fire escape. His pistol thudded onto the carpet, and he slowly turned, hands raised, and looked first into the barrel of a stubby Colt revolver—it had a hammer shroud so that it could be fired from inside a pocket without fouling—and then at the man who held it. He was an

East Indian, straight black hair, sloping Aryan cheeks, hooked nose. The gun was a crazed animal that might bite him, the way he held it with both hands at arms' length. He did not match up to the sophisticated little weapon, looked nervous and hostile. Durell guessed he was about twenty, with rocky shoulders under a grime-impregnated tee shirt. He wore khaki trousers and frayed sneakers.

"Stay where you are," he said thickly.

"I'm not going anywhere."

The thin, angular man licked his lips. The nose of the gun wavered slightly, as if sniffing for Durell's scent, and Durell winced inwardly, aware of a new respect for the theory that East Indians had killed Dick Boyer.

He began to think that this overwrought man aimed to kill him.

It seemed ridiculous, after all the care and preparation, the dedicated and competent enemies that had failed against Durell in the past. Yet, he thought, it came this way sometimes, through a moment of haste, a trifle of carelessness. Unexpectedly. Absurdly.

He watched the man with total concentration, knowing he must attempt to disarm him. But it was highly dangerous.

The man's nerves were on a hair trigger.

Then the shower stopped.

The man's eyes flickered to the bathroom door and back to Durell, and he retreated a step to cover the door. "Who's in there?" he asked.

Durell ignored the question. "We have no quarrel," he said gently. "Did your elders put you up to this? Their grudge is rusty with age."

"What are you talking about?" the man snapped.

Durell stared at him with puzzlement.

The shower door opened, and Durell was reminded that Ana had not known of his plan to vacate the room immediately.

She came out hopeful and sweet-smelling.

Smiling and damp.

Utterly nude.

"Miss Morera!" the man said.

"Have we met?" Ana responded with queenly hauteur.

The man's mouth fell open, the gun barrel drooped, and Durell was at him in one long stride. He snapped the pistol away without resistance, drew a deep, shuddering breath and plucked his .38 from the floor. Ana disappeared into the bathroom with her clothes. The man continued to stare, as if having a vision. Then he turned sad eyes on Durell and spoke with a defeated dignity:

"Forgive me, sir. I have had no work for six months."

"You meant to rob me?"

"Oh, no, sir." He lifted a proud chin. "A man hired me to do this; to come in when he knocked and hold you until he returned. I suppose he won't pay me now. I have a wife and baby daughter—"

"What's the man's name?" Durell interjected.

"Jan Browde. I would not have harmed you, sir."

Durell's face darkened. "So he's coming back. When he comes, you will let him in as planned."

"Yes, sir."

Ana came back into the room, fully dressed this time. An afterthought tinged her cheeks with pink as she turned to the East Indian. "How do you know me?" she asked.

He put on a mannerly smile. "My two brothers work at your plantation. I visit them sometimes with my wife and little baby, who is eight months old. I would not expect you to remember me, of course. I am Ajit Narayan."

"What are you planning to do with him, Sam?" she asked.

"I haven't made up my mind," Durell said. "Maybe I'll give him a job. You go back to the plantation now."

"And miss everything?"

"Just be glad for that," Durell said. "Incidentally, you will have a houseguest tonight—I'll be out later."

Ana smiled. "Marvelous," she said. "Then I won't miss *every*thing."

A couple of minutes after Ana left, Browde knocked and Durell signalled Ajit to let him in. The man was beefy and red-haired, with a florid face and heavy chin. He wasn't young anymore, but he wasn't old, either, and, with crystal blue eyes of stunning force, he had the manner of a top-rated salesman—or confidence man.

He also had a glued-on smirk that evaporated when he saw his own gun in Durell's grasp.

He turned to Ajit and said, "Don't be upset, pal. You did just fine; all that was needed was me getting through the door." Then, to Durell: "I knew you'd only talk over a gun—whichever one of us held it. No harm done, hey? Would you please lower that weapon?"

Durell did not move. "Talk," he said.

"Sure." Browde's voice lowered confidentially, and his eyes scoured Durell's face. "Too bad the cops took that hunk of ice, but there's plenty more where it came from, hey?" He rubbed his hands together. "You know, this is an old porkknockers' town. There aren't many secrets."

Durell was trying to place the man's accent. It resembled middle-class British, but there was the note of a current or former commonwealth country to it.

Browde was saying, "Your late brother-in-law was a friend of Claudius Gibaudan, and the grapevine has it that old Claudius was onto a big shout, a discovery, then just dropped out of sight."

"Meaning?"

"Maybe your brother-in-law had something going with Claudius; maybe it was something you inherited. Simple. Am I on the right track, huh?"

"Where is Claudius?" Durell said.

The smirk crept back to Browde's clever lips. "No one knows. Could it be, Mr. Durell, that your brother-in-law saw opportunity and grasped it—never mind that a worthless old man's neck must come between his fingers in the bargain?"

"You're accusing Dick of murder? To steal Claudius' claim?"

Browde's gesture was disparaging. "Oh, I don't make any accusations. Lordy. That's not my game."

Durell glanced at his wristwatch and spoke with tight impatience. "You have one minute, Browde."

"Certainly. Well—I'll put it bluntly. You have access

to Claudius' diamonds, and I have a connection to dispose of them."

"A buyer?"

"Sure."

"Who?"

"Huh-uh." Browde shook his head and wagged a pink finger.

"I'll only deal with principals," Durell said, his voice flat.

Browde thought a moment. "I'll see what I can set up."

"Tomorrow. In Bartica."

"Isn't that rather out-of-the-way, chum?"

"Take it or leave it."

Durell read his watch again, his thoughts on the police. "Go," he said. "Now."

As Browde went out the door, Ajit moved toward it.

"You stay," Durell said.

He jerked his suitcase from under the bed, yanked it open and threw the stubby Colt revolver down beside the big, dark angle of the Browning, slammed it shut. He waited two minutes by his watch. "Let's get out of this place," he said, and Ajit followed dutifully behind.

As they headed for the stairs, he considered Browde's words. There had been three things of consequence. Dick and Claudius had been friends. Claudius had disappeared, and Dick had been murdered, which could be coincidence, but probably was not.

And, in hopes of finding out more, Durell had just made an underworld contract to deliver diamonds he did not have.

Chapter Thirteen

Durell did not trouble to check out of the Berbice. He slipped down to the rental Fiat and got away from the hotel as quickly as possible. He told Ajit he would pay him well if he would stay at Ana's plantation with his relatives for two or three days, ask the East Indians what they knew of Dick Boyer. He conjectured that if Boyer had made contact with them, Ajit would have less difficulty than he in finding out why. Most of the East Indian community was concentrated on sugar plantations; Ana's was as good as any to start with, and Ajit seemed happy enough with the proposal.

He laughed, and said, "Today I bought a wish from the wish-come-true man, and tonight I found work—twice in a row."

"You were lucky," Durell said.

"Yes, sir. You only run across the wish-come-true man once every three-four years."

Durell made no immediate reply as they passed drainage canals, Ruimveldt Industrial Site, the modern buildings of the Banks Brewery. He did not think they were being followed, but sensed that he was no longer merely the hunter, but the hunted as well.

He told Ajit: "Just don't stir up any hornets."

"Yes, Mr. Durell."

"If you learn anything and can't reach me, don't wait. Call Chad Mitchell at the American Embassy. Chad Mitchell."

"I understand."

Soon they were rolling south on MacKenzie Road through humid farmland, its flat sugar and rice fields and meadows gridded with canals that were pewter under the stars. Palms with enormous shellburst crowns bent and twisted against the trades that rode them. The smell of wet earth brought to mind Louisiana's delta parishes. Durell did not turn as the road to the Morera plantation flashed past. Ajit questioned him against the battering of wind through open windows.

"There's another stop first," was all that Durell said.

They swept on, and the engine's whine shouted back from a village of stilted, peak-roofed houses and high stick fences. The community faucet on a rusty pipe reared beside the road, then the fluttering canvas awnings of a

76

small marketplace, desolate in the night. An abandoned donkey cart. Ditches choked with hyacinths, Azollas, Marsilias and lotus.

Far to the east lightning shot from a billowed mass of black clouds.

Durell slowed, angled the car into a cavernous overhang of trees and vines. The metallic orange of animals' eyes peered from foliage beside the red dirt trail. In places like this, Durell reflected, you could almost believe in the *francup,* a one-eyed giant who eats the unwary; and *duppies,* who cry like children and lead hunters to death in the forest.

Ajit said nothing as he watched the spray of light that advanced ahead of them.

The car rocked and joggled as its tires spun and slewed in the mud.

Abruptly the jungle reeked of dead embers, and Durell's senses tightened.

A last turn into a clearing that was high in weeds, and Durell cut the ignition and stared out the window. Seen through trees to his left was the river, a taut gray skin humming between its banks.

On his right was Peta Gibaudan's shack—or what remained of it. A heap of fire-blackened debris.

Durell regarded the scene grimly. He did not know if the shack had been burned as a warning or as a funeral pyre. He did not know if Peta were dead or alive.

A bubbler frog under the riverbank made a fountain sound over the creakings and sawings of insects. The jungle was impenetrable to sight, shadow layered on shadow.

Durell stepped out of the car, pistol held at waist height, approached the wreckage, sniffed the air.

Ajit stood beside him, distinctly uncomfortable, eyes rolling right and left. "Nobody's here, sir. Don't you think we should go back to Miss Morera's plantation?"

Durell returned to the car on reluctant feet. He felt abruptly weary and remorseful. He'd smelled burned flesh out there.

It might only be a deer haunch, he thought.

Ana's plantation was a one-by-four-mile rectangle coming off the river on its narrow side along lines surveyed by the Dutch more than 250 years before. With the flooding river diked in front and the back-dammed swamps in the rear, existence here was in precarious balance—a microcosm of the world as a whole, Durell reflected. The only relief from several square miles of sugarcane was a grid of ditches, drains and twenty-foot-wide irrigation canals dug by slaves when the land first was reclaimed from pestilential swamps. Where the plantation drive cut through the fields, the cane made oppressive walls twelve to fourteen feet high, and it occurred to Durell that a man might get lost here—or hide—almost as easily as in the jungle.

There was nothing to indicate that he had been followed from Peta's; no evidence to show that harm awaited him where the blackish-green ramparts glimmered past.

But it was difficult to ignore a sense of apprehension that gripped him while the potholed lane continued through the obscuring cane stalks.

He wondered where the men from the *Peerless* were now.

The road opened onto a space where towering palms fussed over an enormous gray-shingled house of Georgian style. Beyond were a barn; a pair of rusty standpipes for household water; and several rows of ramshackle ranges that once housed slaves, but now were quarters for workers' families. Near a confluence of canals, where iron cane barges were tied in a row behind a sluice gate, was a large sugar mill constructed of galvanized steel sheeting—the only building of modern vintage to Durell's view. A huge incinerator smoldered with burning bagasse, the waste of cut, shredded and pressed cane.

Durell drove around the barn, where he parked between a pair of International Harvester farm tractors. Ajit extended his hand in the dark. It was bony and hard. He said, "I shall be alert, Mr. Durell."

"Just stay out of trouble."

Ajit nodded. "You've hired the right man."

"I hope so."

Durell watched him go across the puddle-strewn ground of the ditched and barren workyards to the workers' quarters. A warm scent of forage and manure came through the walls of the barn, and the air was touched by the perfume of hibiscus and water hyacinths. Over all was the sugary fragrance of the mill.

The breeze was chill, the squishy ground flaked with cane chaff, as he strolled to the big house. A light glowed from somewhere deep in its interior. Even considering the hour, the place struck Durell as too quiet, as if holding a secret—or afraid. There was no sound of livestock, no sleepy cluckings, no barking dogs. Even the insects were muted, here in the open. There were only the frogs that peeped and croaked and boomed with distant rancor.

Durell knocked on the door and waited. He could not shake off a sense of unease. Ajit was out of sight. Palm fronds, aluminum under the stars, clashed and gestured high above. The storm cloud, seen earlier from the Mac-Kenzie Road, had disappeared.

Durell tried the door, found it unlocked, pushed it in, his concern for Ana mounting. Abruptly the knob was jerked from his grasp, the door yawned open.

The man who stood in the interior gloom might have been smiling; it was difficult to say.

His face was a ribbed mask of scar tissue.

Chapter Fourteen

There was no time to think.

It was reflex, pure and simple, that urged Durell's shoulder up to protect his neck from a jolting chop; and he knew by the aching impact that the blow was meant to

79

kill. He gripped the arm and twisted. The faceless man flew over his back, crashed against the floor, rolled and bounced onto his feet with steely resilience. In the split-second they faced-off, Durell realized a vague familiarity that went beyond their encounter at the Toucan Patio, something in the black eyes, like volcanic incandescence seen at night. Then the man's booted heel shot out to break Durell's kneecap, missed, ripped painfully down his shin, and Durell reeled against an ebonized wooden cabinet. They grappled with grunts and stifled breath as bric-a-brac rattled and splintered, each seeking the other's weakness with feral speed and merciless efficiency.

Durell sensed now that he was fighting for his life; that this man was good, too good for anything but a deeply experienced professional; and that, moreover, he was enjoying the test of bone and muscle and skill, was in a kind of bloody exhilaration.

Blood dribbled thickly from the noses of both.

Tall as Durell was, the other man was slightly taller, but without Durell's depth of chest. They were evenly matched. Everything depended on skill and daring, quickness and heart.

Suddenly Durell felt the breath squirt from his lungs as the man rammed him with head and shoulder. He was slammed back against the staircase wall, and it shuddered as if struck by a torpedo. Durell thrust his knee low, toward the vulnerable face, felt a satisfying crunch. The man's head popped up, and he staggered back. Durell snatched a razor-edged shard of china and swiped at his opponent's neck, and a red gleam of fear came into eyes that were like black beetles on a shriveled melon. Even hurt and off-balance, the man blocked the blow with a sharp chop to Durell's right wrist that numbed it.

They circled each other cautiously. The man's bloody teeth flashed, and it could have been a grin or a snarl on his pulpy face. Their heavy breathing was the sound of storm surf in the narrow hallway.

It was the first break of sufficient duration to make Durell think he had a chance to reach the .38 in its holster below his right kidney.

He plunged his hand under his coat and became aware too late that the hand still was benumbed, useless to grasp the weapon. His startled thoughts lingered an instant too long on his predicament, and the man charged with an elated grunt, pinning Durell against the wall with only his left hand free. Cabled muscles strained as their bodies flattened together there, the other man with all the advantage. Durell heaved and sweated and smelled garlic and pepper on the other's breath.

His opponent's hand clawed ruthlessly toward the pistol, and they swayed, locked together. Suddenly Durell felt it come free, saw its glint in the dim light, and with a final surge of desperation lobbed his knee into the man's groin. The man yelped, bent, and then Durell's knee caught the side of his head, and he spun away, the pistol tumbling from his hand.

He saw that Durell would beat him to the snub-nosed revolver, chose to run and hurled himself through the door, before Durell could bring the gun to bear in his left hand.

Durell could see nothing out there.

He thought again of the men from the *Peerless*, cursed, slammed the door shut and locked it. Let them come and get him, if they cared to try. He vented a deep breath, rubbed a hand that was beginning to tingle with renewed life.

Then his night-blue eyes moved up the dusky staircase —and there was Ana, her youthful curves sculpted under the flowing drapery of an apricot silk satin nightgown. Her long hair was down now and made rippled black curtains beside her cheeks. Her face was very white.

She spoke his name as if coming out of shock, and she said: "I was asleep—I heard all the commotion— I . . ."

"It's over. All over," Durell soothed. He wiped his nose with his hand, looked at it and asked for a damp cloth. She hurried away and hurried back, the satin whispering, and Durell regarded her with relief. She still was safe. Then his eyes sobered, because he did not know how that could be—unless she'd been a willing partner to the man who had just tried to kill him.

Ana surveyed the damaged hallway, eyes brassy with dismay.

"Why did you attack my foreman?" she asked.

"Your foreman?"

"His room is down here." She strode back and forth through the mess, all of a sudden angry—almost too angry. "I suppose you came barging in and frightened him—I tell him to lock the door, but he never does." Durell just watched her for a long moment.

"You didn't tell him to expect me?" he asked.

"I didn't think it was necessary. It didn't even occur to me."

"Where did you get him?" Durell's voice was quiet.

"Costa Rica." Her slender throat made a pinched sound of vehemence. "You know, some of these things are irreplaceable."

"I'll get a voucher for them. When did you hire him?"

She put her hands on the roundness of her hips. "Money just can't buy them, Sam." Then, abruptly, her irises changed from fire to sugary brown, and she reached up and held his cheeks in her hands, standing close to him, so that he felt the soft, vibrant arches of her body. She sighed. "Never mind," she said in a solemn tone. "Are you all right?"

"When did you get him?" Durell repeated.

She saw the look in his eyes, and her hands dropped away from his face. "Three months ago."

"What do you know about him?"

She spoke rapidly and angrily. "Leon Perez. Forty-six years old. Born near San José, reared on a sugar plantation that was subsequently lost—along with his family—in the eruption of the Irazu volcano in 1963." Her voice turned almost insolent, as she added: "That's how his face got all those terrible scars, if you want to know. Trying to save his wife and children when a cloud of hot ash burned their home. Anything else?"

"How many children?"

"Oh!" she hissed impatiently, eyes glaring.

"How many?" Durell insisted.

"Three, two boys and a girl, four, seven and nine years old. All dead. Along with their mother."

"Of course. So that he didn't have to give you any names. He had the best of both worlds—" Durell spoke sardonically "—he was a family man with all the stability and reliability that implied, but no family to get in the way."

Ana made a shocked sound. "You really think he's involved with the people who killed Dick, don't you."

Durell no longer knew if he could trust Ana, but he was not through with her yet. He took her elbow, and said: "You remember, Ana—I told you about the man who had spied on us at the Toucan Patio?"

Her brown eyes looked at him expectantly.

"Leon was that man," Durell said.

She gasped through trembling fingers. "I don't believe it. Why are you trying to frighten me?"

"I'm only telling you the truth. I'd appreciate it if you'd bring Leon's letters of reference, whatever information he gave you as his employer, up to my bedroom. I hope you will allow me to go through them."

"Well, I—I don't know, Sam. Isn't that confidential?"

"Ordinarily, yes." Durell's smile was unpleasant.

She swallowed, staring at the blue-black eyes. She said, "I'll think it over."

"Don't take too long," Durell said.

"It's breaking a trust."

"You pleaded to help."

She hesitated another second, then went to get the man's file. At least, Durell thought, he could relay the information to Chad to be checked out. He would have to do it immediately, before something else happened. He reckoned more violence was in store; it was just a matter of when, and where—and who survived.

As Ana showed Durell to a bedroom at the top of the stairs, she said: "How about a nightcap? I think I could use one. I'll bring something in."

"Fine," Durell said.

When she was gone, he lifted the telephone and dialed Chad Mitchell's number. As the phone rang and rang, he glanced at his watch, saw it was almost two AM and gave a tired sigh. He had hoped for four or five hours of badly needed sleep, but would dare now only to doze. It would be rest of a sort, anyhow. It was necessary that he get away before dawn—the risk would increase with daylight.

Chad's voice was sleepy and irritable.

Durell said, "I want a background check, Chad. A man named Leon Perez, probably other A.K.A.'s as well, alleged Costa Rican."

"Wasn't in Boyer's files?" Chad asked.

"Would I be calling?"

"Well, goddamn, this time of night and everything, am I supposed to be rational?"

"I need it fast." Durell filled Chad in on the details that Ana had supplied.

"We'll have to tap the computer bank in D.C.," Chad said irascibly. "What about the blackout you ordered on our communications? What about security?"

"What security?" Durell struggled to hold back his anger. "Just send in the clear."

"Look, Sam, that's—"

"Don't argue, Chad. We won't be telling the opposition anything they don't already know. They'll be expecting us to check out Perez now. And tell embassy communications to monitor my receive band from 0600 to 0700 hours—it's K-2, they can look up the frequency in their book. Something should come through in cipher. I'll pick it up from you when I call back about Perez."

Over the line, Durell heard the fizz of a match bursting into flame as Chad lighted a cigarette. "Sam?" The voice was uncertain.

"Yes?"

"Did you *have* to steal Eisler's car? I told you to be careful with him. He's hot under the collar—he's been to the ambassador, Sam. And the ambassador is *most* pissed-off." Chad's voice continued with unaccustomed reasonableness, even pleading: "Now this reflects on me,

Sam, even though I'm supposed to be a diplomat, and K Section was a long time ago, and I happened to get stuck with embassy security through no desire of my own. Sam —please—what do I tell the ambassador?"

"Don't tell him anything," Durell said flatly.

There was an angry pause. Then Chad snarled: "Well, where the hell are you? I'll just tell him and let you handle the questions."

"In a hole, looking out." Durell hung up.

Ana brought glowing golden whiskey in a cut-glass decanter and two matching crystal glasses. As she poured, Durell's eyes ranged around the room, took in the two Demerara windows that looked toward the river, and a jalousied door onto a balcony that ran the full length of the second story. There would be a stairway onto it from the outside. He judged the room to be only marginally defensible, but supposed it was as good as any in the house. It was furnished with a Heal wardrobe inlaid with pewter and ebony, a writing desk decorated with sycamore marquetry, and a comfortable old Morris chair. The bed was a vague reminder of an English galleon, with carved scrollwork on forecastle and poop.

Ana handed a glass to him and raised hers, and her hair swung in a long ebony fan around her shoulders.

"To Dick," Durell said, a remoteness in his eyes.

Ana sipped. Durell tossed down his double and it curled warmly in his stomach. He said: "I brought that Asian here with me, the one who had the gun in the hotel."

"What for?" She sounded dismayed.

"I want him to ask a few questions of your East Indian employees."

"About Dick? They know nothing."

"How can you be sure? I thought I had best tell you; you're likely to see him around."

"But I don't want him here." The moist lower lip of her small mouth swelled with petulance.

Durell eyed her sharply.

"I mean—it's rather embarrassing," she explained, "after the hotel room. Those people are very moral. I'm supposed to set an example. Please—send him away."

"I can't do that," Durell said. He sat heavily on the enormous old bed and kicked off his shoes. "I'd like to rest now. I have to drive to Bartica soon."

"Bartica?" Her face brightened. "I'm going there in the morning, flying up with Calvin. Everybody's going. A new dam is to be dedicated day after tomorrow, 'way out on the Mazaruni, and we're all getting together in Bartica before being shuttled out by air. It'll be fun, parties all night. Come with us."

"Sorry, no," he said. "I'd best stay away from Eisler; I'd advise you to do the same. Especially after tonight."

Her smile was knowing. "He wouldn't blame me for what happened. He doesn't credit me with enough brains to be dangerous. Just because I'm a woman. Isn't that silly?" She watched him over the rim of her glass.

"I won't make that mistake," he said.

"You wouldn't."

She put her glass on the writing desk, and the small reaching movement loosed a silken flow of fabric over her breasts. Durell watched with pleasure, always aware of the sounds of the house, the night noises beyond. This room was a world apart, remote and still—as the eye of a hurricane, he thought.

He said, "You'd better go to your bedroom."

"This is my bedroom." The tapered ends of her fingers touched the wall behind her.

The light went out.

The robe made a whisper like tall wheat around her long legs. Next came a muffled splash as it fell from her shoulders onto the wide planks of the polished floor. She stepped through ingots of starlight, and they leaped from the floor and wiped along her thighs and in the soft roundings and hollows of groin and belly.

She paused, one knee on the bed, arched figure proud as a caryatid. "Do you want me to go now?" she said.

Durell pulled her down, took her in his arms.

"Oh, Sam," she breathed.

"Hush," he said.

He was acutely conscious of the lush gift of her body next to him, her hungry touch, the mingling of freshness and perfume that was her hair and neck—yet the deeper awareness of training and instinct continued functioning unimpaired.

"I've been waiting so long . . ."

"I said be quiet. What's next to this room?"

"The guest room."

He rose, slipped quickly into his shoes.

She rolled onto an elbow, her lovely body streaked with milky light. "Don't go," she said.

"Are there other guests?" His voice was urgent.

Comprehension dawned in her spangled eyes. She drew in a breath, scooped up her robe. Durell did not have to be told more. He crossed the room quickly, urged on by a need for surprise. Ana came behind as he moved quietly down the hallway to the next room.

He swept the .38 S&W from its belt holster and threw open the door. Wooly darkness.

A glint of steel, and he flung himself to one side.

There came the vicious whizz and thud of a knife.

Ana screamed.

Chapter Fifteen

Ana vanished from the corner of Durell's vision.

The knife that protruded from the wall had time to claim only a fragment of his attention, as he hurled himself toward a rangy shadow, withholding his fire.

Something exploded against his head, a pitcher or a table lamp. He hit the floor, saw wizard's images behind his eyes. There was the sound of a swift footfall, a clatter at the jalousied balcony door. He lifted his reeling gaze. Seen briefly against the night sky was a darting blur.

"Peta!" Durell yelled.

He scrambled up, burst onto the balcony. His eyes swung left, then right, reflecting the night. Peta's feet padded down a stairway. Durell took the stairs two at a time, was halfway down, when he heard a running crunch across the lawn.

It seemed insane to follow the Indian youth out there, but Durell had no choice.

He needed the boy desperately.

The half-breed's naked shoulders flashed away in the middle distance, headed toward the sugar mill. Durell vaulted the railing. The solid earth stung his feet. A jacamar burst from hibiscus foliage, its white throat plumage a pale meteor against black shadows. Durell sprinted in pursuit as puddles splashed underfoot.

Leon would be out here somewhere, probably those from the *Peerless* as well. Durell put the thought out of his mind and ran on.

He neared the long star shadows of the double water towers, aware that a dim figure angled toward him from the right. It was not Leon.

"Sir! What happened?"

"What the hell are you doing out here, Ajit?" Durell grabbed the man roughly, pushed him into deeper shadows between the rusty tanks.

"I heard a scream."

"I told you to stay away from trouble."

Durell's breath was ragged and raw in his throat as he glanced at the mill with its smoldering incinerator, then back at the house. A confusion of movement rippled darkly from the barn, surged in his direction.

There were eight, maybe ten men.

Ajit followed his gaze and his eyes went round when he saw the guns that gleamed in their hands.

Durell spoke rapidly: "Get back to the workers' ranges. You're endangering your purpose here."

Ajit ran away, along the dark side of the building. The men were spread out and advancing like skirmishers, at a slow trot, uncertain of their quarry's whereabouts. Durell ducked into the mill.

Red night lamps provided the only illumination in here. Their light scattered weakly against stainless steel vats and white-insulated tanks bound together by ligaments of pipes, electrical conduits, conveyor belts, ladders, raised walkways. Steam clanked and pumps hummed as boilers maintained a low head of pressure through the brief hours of rest. Durell grasped the layout at a sweeping glance. It was similar in all basics to the Louisiana mills he had known in his boyhood.

"Peta," he called, "those men who burned your house are just outside. Let me help you."

His voice mocked him from the high roof and distant walls.

There was little time, and he moved in a hurried crouch past a molasses tank, several large centrifuges, boiling pans. The air was hot and sweet. It would be fiery during the day, heated by simmering cane juices and the equatorial sun on the iron roof.

Durell wondered what kept Leon. He heard nothing to indicate Peta's movement, could not be certain the boy was here, as he continued toward the far end of the mill. He rounded big vessels that were vacuum evaporators and looked past the insulated tank of a juice clarifier. The end of the plant was blocked by heaped cane, a cane feeder table, cutters and shredders, and the long slope of a conveyor that carried bagasse to the incinerator outside.

Something stirred, a shadow of a movement, the barest token of a presence.

And Durell saw that Peta had hidden in a maintenance pit beneath the cane feeder table. He easily could have fled before now, but he awaited Durell's approach with eyes of jade and ruby that showed sullenly under the low red lighting. Durell bent, offered a hand. "Let's get out of here, Peta."

Peta backed away in the darkness of the pit. He looked

dangerous. "You come down," he said in his strange accent, compounded of the Arawak tongue, French and English.

Durell stared at the boy, the tardiness of Leon's pursuit nagging at the back of his mind. He did not know where the man was or what he was up to. He thought of Ana and felt a twist of unease for her. He slid in beside Peta. The candy scent of the mill was mixed here with the odor of grease, and oil dribbled from the machinery low overhead. The rangy youth's coppery skin was bathed in sweat, as if he had run all the way to Ana's plantation, and the scar welts on his arm looked almost fresh and bloody in this light. He carried a simple bag of animal hide, strung over one shoulder.

Durell said, "What do you want, Peta—why did you miss with the knife?"

"Maybe I should not have missed," Peta said. Hostility simmered in the green pans of his irises.

Durell spoke bluntly. "You want the diamond. You were hiding at your house, when Ajit said we were coming here, and you ran after us. You let me catch you now, because you'd rather face me than lose it."

"It's mine!" Peta's eyes narrowed above the sharp blades of his cheekbones, and he lunged for Durell, and Durell swatted him away. Peta's eyes went dull. He shook his head, focused on Durell. "Where is it?" he demanded.

"You must tell me where your father is, Peta."

"I'll tell you nothing. Mr. Boyer said he brought the diamond from my father for me. He was afraid they would catch him, so he hid it."

"Afraid who would catch him?"

"I don't know."

"Where's your father?" Durell repeated.

Peta's answer was a stubborn stare.

Durell regarded the youth with anger and resentment. He would have beaten the information out of him, if he'd thought he could break his will—and if there had been time.

Against all logic, Peta again gathered himself to spring at the more competent and powerful man.

Then he was checked by a voice that called Durell's name.

Durell knew it must be Leon.

Durell peered through the slit beneath the feeder table, saw that it must have been Ajit who slowed his pursuers. If the Asian had been a willing decoy, it had taken his last reserve of courage. He looked whipped and frightened up there in the red shadows of the centrifuges, where Leon held him at gunpoint.

Leon called: "Senor Durell—we caught a coolie-man. He doesn't belong here. Maybe he killed Richard Boyer and was trying for you at the house. I'll turn him over to the police for you, to make up for our misunderstanding. Come out, now."

"Maybe we should do as he says," Peta grumbled.

"Think so? Watch." An aluminum stepladder stood in front of the feeder table, and Durell reached out and tipped it over.

A burst of automatic rifle fire tore savagely at the disturbance, and the ladder jiggled and hopped.

"The only way we'll get out of here alive is to fight our way out," Durell whispered.

"There are many more of them. Can we do it?"

"All we can do is try," Durell said.

He regarded the two men in the dim red distance. Leon held what looked to be a machine pistol with detachable scabbard stock. Ajit stood beside him in the awed slouch of a man at an executioner's post. Durell sweated with concentration, debated the tactics of escape as unseen feet scraped and whispered closer through the gloom. He was urgently aware that time was on the side of the encroaching men, that others would be outdoors, covering the exits. Even in the dark, he viewed an open dash to the Fiat with a sense of dread.

He judged they still did not know his exact location; that he might throw them into confusion, if he could kill their arrogant leader up there by the glistening centrifuges. But now Leon had taken cover behind one of the vessels, his face hardly visible.

It was a slim chance, but Durell decided with misgiving that he must try. He steadied the snub-nosed .38 with both hands and aimed. The light was intolerable, the range impossible, and he might hit Ajit.

He squeezed the trigger; the pistol bucked, and metal sparked and rang as the bullet went wide of the mark.

Slugs slapped, spanged and tore around the feeder table. The racket was ear-splitting, where Durell and Peta hunched in the maintenance well, bits of cane and splinters of lead raining down on them. Peta's lips skinned back and showed teeth clenched against the fury. Durell's guts squeezed with foreboding as the gunfire continued to rage; short, overlapping bursts that moved closer and closer. It was a standard infantry tactic; dart, fire; dart, fire, each man covering the next. They were as well-trained as front-line troops.

Windows crashed. The air seemed hotter, the breathing harder as the barrage raked over them. A relay snapped and a pump hummed nearby with a jarring normalcy.

A heightening sense of urgency told Durell he must slow the advance. He popped his head up, glimpsed, ducked. The gunfire was a wild, stuttering storm, but the fire was unaimed, came from the hip. He steeled himself, abruptly raised his head once more. Bullets whiffed and ricocheted. He quickly aimed and fired, and a pale form slid from atop a tank and thudded among pipes and machinery.

There were no more calls from Leon, only the slap of darting feet, the rattle of automatic rifles.

Peta's eyes slid toward him, and the youth nodded impassively upwards. Durell quenched a brief spark of panic, and his arm levered the .38 high, and it roared. A pink nebula of fluid and fiber burst from the skull of a man on a catwalk, up in the high shadows. He bounced against a railing, sprawled half off the walk, and Durell hoped fervently for his automatic rifle, but it caught in something or was held by a sling.

A sudden quiet descended on the vast, gloomy room.

Peta raised his eyes slowly. "What are they doing?" he whispered.

Durell made no reply. He did not know. He considered the half-breed, saw a black pearl of blood stuck to a splinter wound on his forehead. The boy's poise under threat, his nerveless composure reached beyond his years to millenniums of hunters and what they had learned in the wild about facing danger and overcoming fear. His life, spent on the banks of primitive rivers and dusky jungle paths, had been self-reliant and testing of his courage, and Durell struggled against a rare awareness of kinship that spanned race and time and place.

Durell knew he would sacrifice the young hunter to save himself and his mission, if it came to that. Such choices had been forced on him before, and he had made them without looking back. And yet . . .

He told himself not to think in terms of saving Peta.

The silence rang in Durell's ears, and sweat was acid in his eyes. It was not credible that the loss of two men had taken the fight out of the others.

Something slithered toward them through the ruby shadows.

A steam hose.

Chapter Sixteen

Durell watched with growing alarm as another hose came from a different direction. Now there were three of the things, worming closer.

Nausea spread in Durell's stomach as he realized he was to be boiled alive.

He studied the pit that was to become a scalding vat, mind working furiously. The low bed of the feeder table made upward escape impossible. He could crawl out from under on the other side, but the men were certain to see him lethal seconds before he could reach a door—and,

93

if they did not, there would be the guard beyond it, and another automatic rifle.

He cast frantically about for an element of surprise, something that would delay the men in front and disconcert the man at the door at the same time.

Blubbering water vented darkly from a hose, then another. A fizz, a hiss, and burning white vapor and boiling spray roared and blasted toward them. The racket assaulted Durell's brain, stabbing like a knife. The hoses were rubber-coated coils of steel, easy to shove across the smooth concrete floor, and they inched toward the pit inexorably.

Peta winced, ducked back, clutched at a red patch where steam had touched his shoulder.

The hoses slid into the pit one after another, steel nozzles screaming, steam roiling blindingly, as the temperature of the thickening, reddish air leapt up. Durell captured one of the hoses, pointed it away from the pit. He dared not throw it toward the men for fear its stiff coils would twist back on him and scald his face. Peta followed his example as the rubber casings grew hot, then searing, and the third hose deluged the pit with steam.

There was a shattering roar of gunfire. They released the hoses and ducked as bullets chipped the concrete.

A wave of quick motion rippled down the steamlines as unseen hands straightened them with a jerk. They slid relentlessly back into the pit.

A hellish fire-opal color suffused the boiling cloud. Durell's clothing sopped up the moisture, and it stung his skin. Peta slapped and rubbed where the spray spattered his naked back and legs. They avoided iron rods of steam that would have flayed them instantly, by staying between the hoses. But the heat was crushing, the scorching, sodden air almost impossible to breathe.

And there seemed no way out of it.

Peta never made a sound, just slid to his knees, hands groping weakly at the greasy concrete wall. His head drooped between the bunched muscles of his shoulders, and it seemed to take a last effort to raise his face. His dazed eyes met Durell's with an anguished, despairing plea.

Durell reached for him, slumped onto all fours, coughed and gagged in the live steam.

Then his arms gave way, and he was distantly aware as his chin struck the floor.

The steam kept up its screaming assault.

Durell's body was a dim outline beneath the suffocating stew of vapor. The cloud leaped up to enfold the length of the cane table, then swelled out with ragged, twisting edges until it formed a billowing red curtain of doom from ceiling to floor.

Leon and his men watched from a safe distance, waiting.

The scalding fumes darkened the iron ceiling with condensation; the steel cutting table glistened wetly. Water dribbled and dropped and mixed with the hot water that rushed from the hoses with the steam. The floor of the pit was covered with water.

The water filled Durell's nostrils, and he choked and struggled for breath. He dimly imagined that hot forks jabbed his neck, his back, his hips. He wanted to sink back into the deathly sleep from which he had been aroused. Then he was aware of the water again; aware that he could not breathe. His head jerked up sputtering and snorting. The shrieking of the steam battered his ears; he tried to shake it out of his head. His eyes opened on the dark hell-hole around him.

Remembrance came grimly.

The steam was eating him alive.

His hair swung limply as he raised himself on shaking arms. He knew he would lose consciousness again, unless he got out of here immediately. There was only one hope, and it was a long shot.

He slapped Peta, splashed water on the youth's hot face, slapped him again. Peta moaned, blinked. Durell yanked him from his back to a sitting posture, nerves jangling with a fear that the steam would be cut off too soon, leaving them exposed.

"Crawl out!" Durell shouted over the raging steam.

A weak hand clutched at Durell's shirt. "Where's my diamond? I don't leave without you," Peta said stubbornly.

"You idiot! Do as you're told!"

Durell crawled to the wall of the pit away from the gunmen, raised himself to its brim. Peta was beside him as they wormed through the narrow space between table and floor.

The cool air was like a stiff drink.

Durell's eye caught movement at the nearby door. He had expected that, and scooted his .38 across the floor toward the heavily armed man who stepped into view.

Then he told Peta: "Better put up your hands."

Durell knew that Leon would execute them quickly; that the next few moments would spell escape or death.

The guard fired at the ceiling and the steam roar withered to silence. Durell watched through filaments of mist as shadows approached the long cane table from the other side. He backed half a step unnoticed, bumped the wall lightly, seeking the switchbox for the cane feeder. He kept his hands at shoulder height, and hoped desperately that his elbow would find the switch button on one try.

Peta's sulking eyes clung to the approaching men, as the dim light revealed one, then another, and Leon's scar-mottled face was in their midst. They began scaling the table. One turned and gave Leon a hand up. Durell felt his guts shrink as he looked up into the unforgiving muzzles. He saw few seconds to spare in their hostile eyes. Leon pointed his machine pistol at Durell's face and looked down from his height contemptuously. Durell had thought that would appeal to his vanity, to be able to look down and see him cringing, but Durell did not cringe, and that seemed to anger the man.

"You thought you could stop a revolution single-handed?" Leon rasped. "You are stupid, senor."

Some of the men still were on the other side, but Durell knew time had run out.

His elbow jabbed the ON button.

The cane table's steel-link conveyor belt yanked the feet from under the men up there, and Durell spun on the incredulous guard, his knuckles crushing the man's larynx. Shrieks came from above. Men floundered and were tossed in bewildered terror, while the wide belt hurried them into a hideous whirl of cane chopping knives. Horror seemed to have stunned those on the far side of the table as Durell grabbed the guard's AK assault rifle and heard the flashing knives chunk heavily into a screeching victim.

He rushed out the door, away from the nightmare of jabberings and blood-tinged air. Peta followed as he zigzagged toward the barn.

Mud gushed around them as a flat stutter of gunfire stitched the wind. Peta did not stop running. Durell dived, swiveled, and his rifle hammered at the distant factory door. He caught up with Peta near the car in the night shade of the barn, saw the youth lurch back from the door handle.

"Someone's in there!"

"Wait, Sam! It's just me!" Ana's imploring face shone out the car window. "You're not ditching me now. What took you so long?"

"Get your head down," Durell barked. He fired a last burst at the mill, spent cartridges making a chain in the air, then jumped behind the wheel. Peta scrambled into the rear seat, the door still open as the car spun around the barn and lurched onto the cane-walled lane by which, it seemed, Durell had arrived a century ago.

He rued the forfeit of Ajit—it had not been that one's lucky night, after all. But he could not remain effective in the business and brood about the losses, he thought darkly.

Ana drew a sharp breath.

And, at the same time, Durell felt the steely snout of a gun against the back of his head.

Part of Durell's mind stood objectively aside and noted that Peta, with remarkable restraint, had kept a gun hidden, doubtlessly in the leather pouch, through everything that had happened in the mill, chancing capture, possibly torture, certainly death, anticipating a moment when he could use it on Durell and be reasonably certain of a safe escape. The other part of Durell's mind stormed with anger and dismay, but he kept his voice calm, as he said: "Why didn't you use that when it was needed, Peta?"

"Against them? It would have made no difference— but here, it does." The boy's voice tightened. "I wish you no harm, Mr. Durell. You are very much of a man, and a good man, I think. Just tell me where my diamond is."

The car did not slow in its flight through the wind-stroked cane. Ana's face was as pale as the tropical starshine. Oddly enough, she had not asked what diamond, but maybe she was too frightened.

Finally, Durell replied: "If you pull that trigger, Peta, you'll never know."

He felt the gun go uncertainly away from his skull, and added: "I guess you're along for the ride—all the way."

Durell's hands trembled slightly. Adrenaline. Weariness. Anticipation. And his clothing was a chill mess that grated soggily on patches of tender skin.

But he was on the road to Bartica, on the track of the Warakabra Tiger. Rapidly, his thoughts ordered themselves into a list. All he had to do was:

Hope that Peta would tell him how to find Claudius.

Go through the motions of selling a diamond he did not have, under the nose of Peta, who would try to kill him if he knew.

Get a look inside Dick's police-sealed house, even as the police sought his arrest and deportation.

Check the Chinese dam in the face of Colonel Su's warning not to venture there.

And then, remembering Leon's words, attempt to stop a revolution single-handedly.

Chapter Seventeen

"You won't let Peta keep that gun, will you?" Ana said.

"I'm not going to take it away from him," Durell replied.

"You're afraid you'll have to harm him?"

"Maybe."

"Why do you protect him?"

"I need him."

Ana sighed, sat back, folded long, narrow hands in the lap of a raincoat she had thrown over her apricot silk gown. Durell noted she'd had the presence of mind to pack a suitcase. It filled half of the cavity between seats, crowding Peta, whose resentful green eyes paced back and forth, from Durell to Ana, never resting.

Distant headlamps flared above the cane just as they turned from the plantation road onto the highway, and Durell knew they were being pursued. Thankful for the AK rifle beside him, he put his foot to the floorboard and drove with one eye on the rear-vision mirror. The little car split through the spanking wind, and the palms did a witch's dance against the sky.

A ferry took them across the Demerara to Vreed en Hoop, and they dashed around a long curve of the shore to Parika, where the highway ended at another red-dirt trail gouged through the jungle. It paralleled the Essequibo River, Guyana's mightiest stream, whose headwaters mingled near the green-shrouded Akarai Mountains with tributaries of the Amazon. Durell caught Ana's apprehensive glance and let up on the gas as the Fiat rocked and banged over ruts. They had gained a comfortable margin of time at the ferry, but if anything happened to the car, their lead could evaporate—and there was nowhere to turn but the alien jungle or the impossibly wide and swift Essequibo.

"What do you think, Peta?" Durell asked. "Will the road be passable to Bartica?"

"This time of year?" Peta's words were thoughtful. "I think so. I have traveled it this season. But that was in a truck, with Mr. Eisler." The low light of the dash patinized his coppery face as it swung toward the river, and something like fondness softened the points of his green eyes. "Alone, I go on the river, instead of this road," he said. "I have been its length, past Watu Falls. I know it like the Kwitaro, the Rupununi and the Potaro, where the Patamona tell of their great chief Kai."

"What was so great about Kai?" Ana asked. Her tone suggested that she expected to be amused, and her smile was flippant.

Peta's face darkened. He said nothing.

"You've heard of Kaiteur Falls," Durell supplied, the steering wheel jerking in his grip.

"Of course—five times higher than Niagara, for whatever that's worth."

"Legend says that Kai sacrificed himself by canoeing over the falls in hopes that Makonaima, the Great Spirit, would save his tribe from the Caribishi cannibals."

"Did it work?" Ana asked.

"As Peta said, the Patamona are still with us."

"We could use a Kai now." She turned, put a casual hand on Peta's rough knee. "Would you be my Kai, Peta? Would you sacrifice yourself to save me from those awful men?"

"Shut up and leave the boy alone," Durell snapped.

Peta said, "I will help you, if I can." He looked at the hand on his knee as if it were a rare bird, and his eyes shone on Ana with a light of new possibilities and on Durell with increased resentment. "Don't tell her to shut up," he said.

Durell understood that Ana was different from the short-breasted and stubby girls of Peta's native village; a rarity to the boy's experience among hard-faced harlots of porkknockers' dens. The look in Peta's eyes said she was the most beautiful being he'd ever seen, with the white sweetness of delicate kakaralli flowers, the grace of a jaguar. Durell saw clearly that Peta was a little afraid of her touch, that he struggled to keep his fierce pride at a safe distance.

Then a yawn curled Ana's sharp little nose, and she turned to Durell and said: "What's next, Sam? What do we do in Bartica?"

"You go with Eisler to the dedication of the dam; I take care of my business."

He glanced back. The darkness behind on the jungle trail was complete. Freckles of starshine swarmed in the black overlap of trees above. Not even that much sky would be visible a few yards to either side of the road. Now and then the road bent close to the river, and the water was a brief flash of platinum. Suddenly something like a rough log shone across the ruts, and the little car crashed and leaped over a cayman.

"You don't mean we're splitting up in Bartica, Sam?"

"Exactly." Durell's tone was blunt.

"Why?"

"You have no more place in this."

Ana's face turned petulant. "You mean you have no more need of me. Maybe I can show you differently, given the chance."

"Put it however you like," Durell said. A gentle note came into his voice. "You're an amateur, Ana. You might get yourself killed. You might get me killed."

"But what about Dick? He was my friend. You said I could help."

"And you have. That's enough."

Peta's voice came low and solid from the rear. "Mr. Boyer was my friend, too. And my father's." He lifted his pistol, and added, "I will use this on whoever harmed Mr. Boyer—and, if they've harmed my father . . ." He left the sentence hanging over an abyss of menace.

Ana tossed her hair and turned to the youth. "Maybe we should team up, Peta. We'd show the Cajun a thing or two. What do you think?" She smiled.

Peta gazed at her out of the sides of his eyes.

The road turned progressively worse. The potholes became long, yellow pools, and large branches snarled with flowering lianes formed obstructions that had to be moved. Durell was glad the rainy season just ending had not brought down whole trees. The tires mired to the hubcaps, and Durell and Peta put limbs under them and heaved and sweated, while Ana gunned the engine.

It was less than forty miles to Bartica, but they had made only half the distance in two hours. Durell saw why guests for the dedication chose to fly. Then something caught his eyes on the right, beyond the trees. He stopped the car and surveyed what appeared to be a river camp a few yards away.

"We'll try to get some rest," he said, and turned the car onto a trail. It was overgrown with young sawgrass two feet high, and little river bats fluttered in the headlamp beams. The lights spun a large lean-to out of the darkness. Durell parked behind it, out of sight of the road. The ground was soft underfoot, a wet clay overlaid with a rotting corduroy of thin logs. Below the riverbank, sand and pebbles formed a narrow beach, recently uncovered by the falling water level. A boat dock stood three feet above the surface, which would drop another three yards, Peta said, before the dry season ended.

Peta walked about with a knowing air, his gun now in the leather bag strapped over a shoulder. He sniffed and poked and told them to watch out for scorpions under the rotting logs. The big scorpions—some six inches long —were not the worst, he said. The worst stings came from the tiny gray ones, and there were many more of those.

Finally he said, "This is Manatee Point. We're first here after the rains," and seemed satisfied that he had said enough.

They built a smudgy fire inside the lean-to, taking care that its glow did not reach the road, and, by its low, waffling light, strung up three of the hammocks that had been left hanging coiled in a corner. There came a tremendous smack from the water nearby, and Ana jumped.

Peta grinned and said, "Just a cayman calling fish,

Miss Morera, or a big *lau-lau* catfish, come up and slap his tail."

Ana's sugar-brown eyes showed no comfort. She insisted on dressing before lying down, and Peta and Durell stood behind the lean-to while she changed into cotton slacks, high lace-up boots and a safari jacket.

Durell wondered where Leon's men were. Maybe they had turned back at the ferry; maybe they hadn't. "We'll stay here three hours, each taking an hour's watch and getting two hours' sleep," he said. He spoke to Peta: "You take the first watch down by the road. Keep out of sight, and, if anything stops—"

"I'll let you know," Peta said. He went into the snatching shadows, the low grass silent beneath his feet.

Durell filled a rusty tin can with water and snuffed out the fire with it, then collected the AK rifle from the car and crawled into a hammock, the rifle beside him. The river sang and threw sparks of white fire, seen beyond the ebony outline of a monkey pipe tree that smelled of jasmine and cast pale cream flowers. The overtowering jungle assaulted the ears with a thousand sounds, made more intense by the darkness of the moldering shelter.

"Sam?" Ana's hammock squeaked at its knots. "Sam, if you turned back now . . ."

"Not a chance, Ana."

The predawn breath of the forest chilled Ana, as her long legs swung out of the hammock, and she made her way toward the slatted luster of the river. The loom of enormous trees dwarfed the little clearing and rained an irregular patter of leaves, twigs, fruit that mixed with the purling of the current, the dainty crush of Ana's boots. She went carefully, hips, knees loose and yielding to the bumps and dips on the hidden earth; eyes wary in a face of faint radiance; long hair an invisible flow in the dark.

She did not know exactly where Peta was.

She was certain she would find him down here, bathing in water that flowed like liquid silver from distant mountain vaults.

Her pulse quickened at the thought of his hard, young

body, and her tongue ran a predatory tip around her small mouth. She did not care to dwell on that; put it out of her mind. That would take care of itself, she reflected as she slid the last few feet down the grassy bank to the beach. The air was thick as honey and smelled of dew-bent flowers. The night shouted with stars.

Her clothing was tight and damp, uncomfortable around her waist and at the knees and armpits. She walked silently, slowly down the beach, unbuttoning her blouse as she went, the sparkled brass of her eyes searching the sand, then rising to the distance or turning back over her shoulder.

She did not think Sam had seen her leave.

He was down by the road, where he had relieved Peta. He had risen from his hammock with slow reluctance, looking tired in gait and posture. Poor Sam. He should have married Deirdre and got out of the business. But he was a legend and would never quit, not until he was dead, she thought sadly.

Abruptly she pulled the tail of her blouse from under her belt and smiled to herself. The chill was invigorating, liberating as it crept over the roundness of her pointed breasts, her ribs and stomach. She unbuckled her heavy leather belt, wondering again of Peta, and thinking she knew how he would respond. Her excitement tingled in her chest, pulsed at the side of her neck.

She had never killed before.

She regretted it—but Peta was really too dangerous to let live.

She had expected to be afraid, but fear did not come. Only a heady anticipation.

The air was delicious against her tawny skin as she untied her boots and stepped out of her slacks. It was like being stroked with mittens of cool fur, she thought, and she made a purring sound in her throat. She closed her eyes and pursed her lips, face upturned, as if to kiss the sky.

Then the stars tracked a shadow of lithe limbs and swinging breasts, as she moved on down the damp sand. Branches rattled where they overhung the water a few yards ahead, and Ana knew that would be Peta, coming back this way. She felt fully competent against the youth. He was little more than the animals that crept through forest trails beyond the shoulder-high riverbank. They scavenged on the fringes of the modern world, obsolete and outmoded—or worse, got in the way of real people and societies.

She must get him near her—on her—to be sure of the kill.

The thought blew a hot, erotic breath across her loins, and her heart quickened. Peta moved with dark, lean grace around the fronds ahead, the river frothing in white bands at his thighs, face turned down toward the water, as if lost in thought. The long muscles of his naked body rippled under a sheen of starlight as he splashed onto the sand.

As Ana had expected, he carried his leather pouch with him.

Her resolve slackened briefly when his face turned toward her and he stood still. But then she smiled inwardly at the spectacle of the stupid boy frozen to the spot. That's right, she told herself: stupid boy. Dead boy. Building up her hatred and, oddly, she noted, her lust. He *was* beautiful.

Then she spoke, her voice light in the huge wilderness space: "Come here, Peta."

"What—what do you want?" He did not move.

"What do you think I want, silly?"

"Leave me alone." Peta's green eyes flashed, and he shook his head.

"You might like it, Peta. You just really might like it, you know." She lifted her long hands, and her breasts rose.

"Mr. Durell will be angry."

"Are you afraid, Peta? Well, if you are afraid . . ."

Peta crossed the shadow-strewn space and looked obliquely at her. She held out a hand. His grasp was tentative. She arched her neck and looked beyond him at the million stars that hung above river and jungle, and put his dark fingers on her breast. She did not look at him; he was merely a shadow closing around her as his

105

arms embraced her, and she bent her knees and pulled him down on the cool sand.

His body was a hot, trembling urgency, and Ana was startled to feel herself respond physically. Yet her mind was detached, distant, up there with the Southern Cross, blazing in its clarity.

Her hand sought the mouth of the leather bag.

The Tokarev was heavy, brutish in her grasp, as Peta struggled atop her.

Ana's detachment suddenly shattered, and she squirmed to avoid him and brought the big pistol, awkward and outsized in her delicate hand, toward Peta's oblivious head.

Now she was in a hurry. It had gone on too long; she'd carried it too far. . . .

Peta buried his face into her lovely neck, uncaring as she heaved to throw him away. Her mind was a tumult of fear and desperation, her rushing breath dry behind her teeth.

She raised the gun to Peta's temple—

Chapter Eighteen

Durell knocked the gun from Ana's hand, heard a chirp of pain, threw Peta sprawling in the sand. Peta came up on the balls of his feet and just stood there, naked, dazed, ribs heaving.

"Get back to the camp. Get some clothes on," Durell said.

Ana's tawny arms clenched Durell, and she sobbed against his chest. Durell grasped her shoulders, pushed her back a step, saw Peta disappear into the brush.

"Aren't you going to *do* anything?" Ana demanded.

"Voices carry in this damp air," Durell replied. Ana's face went down, and Durell pushed it back up, a finger under her chin. Reflections from the water made a silken net across her breasts and stomach. "Why did you do it, Ana?" he said, his voice rough.

"I came to get his gun." Her eyes flared. "He shouldn't have that gun, Sam!"

"Another second and you would have killed him." Durell wanted to hit her.

"He threatened you with it—"

"And I told you I needed him." Durell slapped her with a short blow, saving most of his strength from harming her, and she fell against him. "Don't help me anymore, Ana," he said.

Ana clung to him, whimpering. "I'm sorry. It was awful. Not like . . . . " Tears starred her eyes as she turned her face up to him, and he felt the urgent press of her body against his. "Not like—if it were us."

Durell stared down at her and did not move. She was more of a stranger now than on their first encounter, standing here naked as a snake.

Ana's arms tightened around him, and she spoke rapidly, her voice thin. "Sam—Sam, darling. Please, make it like it would have been at my house."

Durell twisted away from her, found the Tokarev. He threw it into the river and admitted to himself that he felt better with it gone.

"I've got to find Peta," he said.

As he topped the riverbank, he glanced back. Ana stood watching him, hands on rounded hips, fire shining in her brassy eyes.

For long moments of worry, Durell thought Peta had run away. He was not in the lean-to; he did not respond to Durell's calls. Durell found him sulking in the Fiat. They exchanged brief stares. Durell spoke first. "You shouldn't have gone to the river. I might have needed you."

"I wanted to bathe."

Durell heaved a breath, rested his hands on the damp car roof. "We've got a job to do, Peta. I thought you could hold up your end of it."

"Don't speak to me like a child."

"I'll take you for a man when you can be depended on as one."

"I showed Miss Morera I was a man."

Durell gazed at the youth's hooded eyes. "Son, there are dangers in this world you never guessed. In the jungle you know what is real, and what is shadow. You must learn the same distinctions in people."

"How?"

"Start by keeping your distance from Ana."

"She likes me."

"That's a shadow."

"You're jealous."

"She might have killed you with that gun."

"What gun?"

Durell stared at him. "Just look in your pouch," he said and turned angrily away. There was no point in arguing it. Peta would only find a way to rationalize what had happened and end by insisting he could take care of himself.

It would be harder than ever now to win his cooperation, Durell decided.

But he would have to have it this day.

Bartica was two more hours away, hours of grinding driving, clearing the road of fallen debris, heaving and pushing at the rear of the little car. Ana ignored Peta, and the Indian youth grew sullen. Durell kept his eye on both of them.

The first light of dawn colored the sky copper as they drove at last into Makouria and were ferried to Bartica. The day heated rapidly, and a crochet of mist lifted from the Essequibo, an oily, sizzling flood of silver and tea-brown, iron-gray and violet that was four miles wide below Bartica. Three miles west of town the Mazaruni and Cuyuni rivers joined before spilling into the Essequibo, and the mingling of waters was enormous at the hill-crowned point of the town. Motorboats buzzed to and from riverside houses; timber rafts floated down from distant concessions headed for ocean-going steamers waiting at Kaow Island; an old trading launch carried a few diamond and gold prospectors, bananas and salted fish.

Bartica was the jumping-off place for the interior, an indispensable port of call during the gold rush early in the century. The increasing use of aircraft had diminished that importance, but Durell noted that it still bustled with traders and humming sawmills. Men of every race moved among donkeys, goats, chickens and dogs in its dusty streets, many of them porkknockers, baleta bleeders and woodcutters with machetes or cutlasses hanging from their belts. Most of its houses had rusting tin roofs, and the forest towered over its fringes and the river banks on all sides.

Durell spoke to Ana. "Which hotel has your reservation?"

"Let me stay with you, Sam."

"Which hotel?"

"I know I was wrong to do that with Peta. Don't hold it against me."

Durell stopped the car. Down amid mooring poles washerwomen sang and scrubbed clothes on big greenheart logs. A giant blue butterfly wafted through the air. The sun pained the eyes and a dark sweat stain had begun spreading across Durell's shirt. He was in no mood for debate.

"Get out of the car," he said.

"Here?" Ana glanced about. "What for?"

"It's the end of the line."

Ana regarded his grim stare. "All right," she said, and made a moue with her provocative little mouth. "You win. Take me to the Baro-tika Hotel, over on Second Street."

Durell told Peta to wait in the car, while he carried Ana's bag into the old hotel. A few dignitaries already were here and stood about the lobby chatting with the air of conventioneers between seminars. The bar was open, but honest working men disdained it now, and it was depressing with unaccustomed propriety.

Durell dropped Ana's bag in front of the polished splendor of the mahogany main desk, and his gaze mingled briefly with Ana's. He decided there was a reflection of relief in her sugary eyes, after all.

"Be seeing you, Sam," she said.

He nodded. They did not touch. He turned and walked away.

As she stepped onto the shaded porch, Otelo Antunes strolled toward him. A supercilious smile twisted his thin lips. He was dressed in a smart suit of lightweight gray cloth, and his black eyes were slick with self-satisfaction.

"Ah, Mr. Durell." A big hand went for the steno pad in his pocket. "You're to be a guest at the dedication, I presume?"

"You presume?" Durell started to turn away.

"Unless you're here on K Section business."

Durell wondered how long Otelo had known this; how he had found out. But he did not wish a public discussion of the subject. He paused and said in a low voice: "Stay away from me. Don't think you can be lucky twice."

"It's you who will need luck, after tomorrow."

"You've written a story?"

"And turned it in to my editors, Mr. Durell. It's already being set in type for publication tomorrow afternoon."

Durell's face did not change, as he said: "Thanks for the warning. That gives me a little more than twenty-four hours."

"Better enjoy them, Cajun, because then your life will be worthless, to judge by what happened to Mr. Boyer."

Durell did not bother to reply. He knew Otelo was just a tool. He left the newsman standing there and went back to the car, aware that his usefulness would be ended after tomorrow—even if he could save his life.

Chapter Nineteen

"Where are we going?" Peta asked.

"To the seaplane landing. I'll have to charter a plane to take us up the Mazaruni this afternoon."

"I do not want to go," Peta said.

"Neither do I."

"That country belongs to the Warakabra Tiger."

"Your father's claim is there, isn't it?"

"I won't tell you."

"You'll have to take me, Peta. I've a hunch Dick was there. All I can do is follow his trail."

"Will you give me my diamond?"

"When I can."

Peta sat far back in a corner of the car, arms folded, sunlight fatty white on the scar welts of his arm. They passed fishermen in straw hats repairing nets down by the water. Black smoke from the town's electrical generating plant spoiled a brilliant sky that was dotted with small white clouds. The clouds drifted from horizon to horizon and bore blue shadows across the river and simmering jungle.

Peta watched the great band of water stretched north toward the sea, and said: "My father was a criminal. They put him on Devil's Island, and he never went back to his home."

Durell made no reply, eyes on the road as they wound past the crumbling river wall.

"My father told me how they buried the dead," Peta resumed. "They took them onto the ocean in a small boat, and, when they reached a certain place, they rang a bell. All the sharks came to the boat. Then they threw the dead overboard. The sharks knew what the bell meant."

There was another long pause, then Peta said: "My father had a fear of being fed to the sharks like that. Now I'm afraid the Warakabra Tiger has eaten him."

"He may be alive, Peta. He may know more about the Warakabra Tiger than anyone. You've got to help me find him."

Peta spoke angrily. "So you can steal the rest of his diamonds? Maybe to give to your fancy woman, Miss Morera?"

"I didn't steal your diamond; the police took it."

"You lie. If I had the diamond, Miss Morera would see who is generous."

"Talk of generosity after you find the courage to help your father," Durell said.

He parked beside the landing where two small floatplanes were tied up at a long dock of weathered planks. A man with sunlight glancing from his aviator's sunglasses inspected the left pontoon of a Cessna. Scores of steel fuel drums were scattered about here, and the jungleriver scent reeked of gasoline.

Durell and Peta descended steps cut from the earth of the riverbank and topped with wide boards. Water wrinkled away from the floating dock as they walked out to the planes.

The pilot was a young man with an enormous blond mustache that curled at the ends. He had a short, solid build and a broad head with a crooked nose, and reminded Durell of a prize fighter.

"Hey, you an American?" he asked, when Durell spoke.

"Don't spread it around."

"Tourist?"

"Can you fly us up the Mazaruni this afternoon?"

"Whereabouts? Mazaruni's a mighty long river." The man had a Southwestern accent.

"That new Chinese dam would be fine."

"Just looking around, huh?" The man grinned, but Durell could not see his eyes through the glasses. "You don't look like a tourist."

"Do you want the job or not?"

The man wiped his mustache and spat into the river. "Nope. Don't think so. Plenty of business between here and Georgetown today. Lots of work tomorrow, too. How about the day after?"

"It's got to be today," Durell said. "I'll pay you seventy-five."

The smoked lenses peered at Durell. "Tell you what: make it a hundred, and I'm yours. I could pick up more on the shuttle to Georgetown, but these muckety-mucks just make me tired."

"You've got it," Durell said.

"When you're ready to take off, you can find me here or over at the Kyk-over-al Hotel, my favorite flea-bag. Just ask for Rick Kirby." The pilot shook hands with Durell and strode away.

Durell folded the stock of the AK, put the weapon in his suitcase, then stowed the suitcase in the red and blue airplane. Then he had Peta show him to Dick's riverside shack, found its shutters closed and door boarded up, and decided to wait for midafternoon to break in. Nearly everybody napped after lunch, and there would be less risk of being seen. Next, he drove out of town and pushed the Fiat over a high bluff into the river. With it out of the way, the police—or Leon's agents—were less likely to spot him, he decided.

It meant he had burned yet another bridge behind.

For a man with no option of turning back, it hardly mattered.

He felt a nagging worry about the police, and chose a hotel in a run-down section of town by the Mazaruni River for a rest. It was near an open market that gleamed with oranges and mangos and fresh river fish. Across its dilapidated front was a sign so weatherworn as to be hardly legible: TWO GENTLEMEN. Lettering of more recent vintage stated that rooms were available by the day, week or month. Two domino games were in progress on the front porch, and men smirched with jungle mud came and went through the front door with glasses of rum and beer.

It was the next step above the loggias, open-sided, mud-and-thatch lodgings where you could sling your hammock for a few pennies a day, and Durell judged that the police kept clear of it.

Inside, Durell guessed by the dingy elegance of faded damask drapes that the place had been successful enough during the gold rush days. Its ceiling fans twisted slowly, stirring the growing weight of hot, humid air, and potted rubber plants and palms showed dead brown spots under fine red dust.

They had food brought to their room, where another ceiling fan turned listlessly, and a mild stench of fishguts crept up from the riverbank. Durell ate lavishly of fried steak and *metemgee*, a delicious concoction of edoes, yams, cassava and plantains cooked with coconut milk and grated coconut. Peta had fish and pepperpot. "I was never in such a place," he said, and poked a chunk of fish into his mouth with his fingers.

"It's a big world. You may see a lot of it, if your father has struck it rich," Durell said.

"He was due back last week. Something has happened to him."

"We will see," Durell said.

They ate in silence and waved away the flies. Then Peta said, "If I were rich, Miss Morera would like me even better."

"Ana is not for you, son. Put her out of your mind."

"You want her." Peta's eyes narrowed to slits of jungle-green.

Durell ignored the challenge and shook his head in silence. Peta simply refused to recognize the menace she had been to him. Durell sensed he had earned only increased hatred and suspicion by his intervention. He recalled the scene on the sand, the struggling bodies, the raised pistol—he wondered if Ana could have pulled the trigger. She had done enough damage as it was. Peta's cooperation seemed further away than ever.

He thought he might try to force it, but the kid was strong-willed, and pressuring him too much could backfire.

His best hope, he decided, lay in Peta's concern for

Claudius. Once the boy made up his mind to go for his father, the tables would be turned: Peta would realize that only Durell could help him then.

Durell peered through the slats of the windows, then checked the hallway. Everything appeared to be normal. "We'd better get some sleep, now," he said. "I don't know when there will be another chance."

Peta pushed back his empty plate, licked his fingers, gave a lazy yawn. "I don't like it in here. It stinks of people. I'll sleep on the veranda," he said. He took a rush mat from the floor and tossed it onto the shady veranda and closed the door.

The sun went under a cloud as Durell waited a moment, then moved to the telephone and placed a Georgetown call with an indifferent operator. His room had not been reserved, and he regarded the risk of a tapped line as nil. Troubled winds fluttered against the steel-gray river, seen through the window, and an abrupt rush of air cooled the room.

The receiver emitted impatient whistles, made kissing sounds against his ear.

Then the tin roof rattled as if under a curtain of chains, fell briefly silent, resumed with furious noise under the rain shower's solid impact.

Someone answered, a clerk or secretary, impersonal and businesslike. The call was switched to Mr. Mitchell.

"Chad? What do you have? This is an open line, so make it quick."

"Your sub appears to be headed for Cuba, Sam."

"And Perez?"

"Nothing has come through on him."

Durell swore. He'd hoped for confirmation that Leon was a foreign agent bent on the destruction of the government. With that he might have convinced the Guyana Defense Force to furnish commandos to go into the jungle with him. Now that was out. He had only himself and whatever use he could make of the reluctant Peta.

He spoke over the pounding rain. "Otelo Antunes just bragged that his paper will break a story tomorrow naming me as a K Section agent."

"That son of a bitch. That means the same thing could

115

happen to you that happened to Boyer. You'd better get to the safety of the embassy while you can."

"They'd like that. You'll have to try to stop publication."

"What if I can't?"

"I move ahead, one way or the other."

Durell replaced the phone in its cradle, rubbed the stubble that had begun to show on his chin. At least he could assume that Cubans were involved here. It came as no surprise—Cuba was the logical jumping-off place for revolution in Latin America.

Now he had to consider the possibility that there was a connection between the Cubans and the Warakabra Tiger that terrorized the far reaches of the jungle.

The question was how—and why.

He lay down, hoping for a brief sleep.

The hot air siphoned sweat from his pores, and the bedspread turned moist under his back. Thoughts tumbled roughly through his mind, without order in his drowsiness, thoughts of Ana and Otelo and Leon—thoughts of a continent on the brink of bloody revolution.

His hand rested on the pistol beside him, and the rotating ceiling fan became hideous cane-cutting knives that whirled gore, and he was looking against his wish to see if Leon was amid the slivered flesh.

The chopping knives sounded against his ears: *chunk, chunk!*

His eyes opened, and the sound turned to a knocking at the door.

Chapter Twenty

Durell dropped his feet silently to the floor, was aware of runnels of sweat on his face, a coolness on his back, where the air struck the damp plaster of his shirt. Bushes and vines buzzed and whined with rancorous insect voices out there under the blistering sun. Dusty spears of sunlight stabbed at the eroded old floor from the west now, and he did not know how long he had slept. The room was stifling, his mouth dry, his mind fevered.

He let out a slow breath, and his snub-nosed gun pointed toward the door.

"It's me—Browde. Are you there?" The whisper was urgent. The doorknob turned slowly.

"Hold it," Durell said. He unlatched the door. "Come in."

Browde closed the door behind him, flopped in a creaky rattan chair. He wore white shoes and a white linen suit with an open-necked blue shirt that matched the color of his probing eyes. His face was almost scarlet from the sun, and sweat ran down his thick neck. "Some dump you got here," he said, and a sigh puffed out his cheeks. "I had to look all over for you."

"You didn't bring anyone with you?"

"Not here, pal."

"Where, then?"

"They're waiting. You got the diamonds?"

"What do you get out of this?"

"What's it to you, chum?"

Durell's cheeks hardened, and his eyes turned hostile. He wondered if Browde had a gun under his coat. The room stank as the heat of day cooked odors of old sweat and filth out of musty closet and grimy mattress. He smelled sewage that had been dumped into the purling river.

Browde surrendered to his dark gaze, lifted his palms. "All right, I bring interested parties together. You might call me a producer. For that I get five percent—off their end, not yours. Fair enough?"

"Who are the buyers?"

"You make me nervous, chum." Browde wiped his forehead, a limp handkerchief passing across his eyes.

"Answer my question."

"Some Brazilian Portuguese," he said vaguely. "Middle

117

level. Ties to the diamond pirates. Who the boss is, I don't know."

Durell regarded him with thoughtful scrutiny. He switched the gun to his other hand, wiped a wet palm against his trousers, switched the gun back. "Names," he said.

"No names, chum." Browde's eyes went gritty.

Durell decided not to push it. "Tell me about the diamond pirates," he said.

"They operate all over the interior. There's no effective police presence out there. They trade for stones, buying them cheap and selling their goods dear. They smuggle the diamonds out of the country, avoiding taxes and export duties here and taxes and import duties at the destination. That way they can undercut the international price set every year by the De Beers syndicate's Central Selling Organization in London—and there's a hot market for their stones all over the world. The porkknockers couldn't care less: they trade for guns, ammo, provisions, whatever they need, without the bother of trekking out of the wilderness. They know the diamond pirates cheat them, but it's better than taking a month to go to the outside and back—many of them don't see civilization for three or four years at a stretch, and don't care to."

"Don't the pirates ever jump claims?" Durell was thinking of Claudius.

"Of course, when they can. But that is not often."

"Why?"

"The porkknockers take care to conduct their business in neutral territory, at least a day from their digs—they know better than to trust the pirates at their claims."

"But I'm supposed to trust them?"

"You've got the same choice the porkknockers have, my friend. Sell your diamonds to legitimate dealers—if you can explain where you got them."

Durell thought about it for a moment. He had no diamonds to sell, but he could not worry about that now. Browde's pals might have valuable knowledge about what was going on in the diamond district.

"Where do I find your friends?" he said.

"They will be waiting, down by the river. Go west on the street out front. Takes you right there. An abandoned sawmill, the last one at the end of the path."

"I'll be there in fifteen minutes," Durell said.

"It's a deal" Browde bounced from his chair, held out a hand.

Durell waved his gun toward the door.

Browde dropped his hand, a frown clouding his face.

Durell made a sharp motion with the gun.

"All right, I'm going," Browde said.

Durell locked the door, turned, saw Peta just as the youth dived for him.

Durell took the half-breed's weight across his hip and flipped him head over heels. Peta's hard fingers scrabbled at the floor, and he found his footing and leaped again. The back of Durell's fist hurled him against a wall, and he slid down, panting. Durell's training and experience were one with the muscle and sinew that moved against the boy in easy, effortless precision, the mind and body a single entity. He had not drawn a heavy breath.

Peta was on his knees, head swaying loosely back and forth, dazed eyes on the floor. "I heard you talk to that man," he said above ragged breathing.

"I know. I expected you would."

"You lied; you said the police have my diamond."

"They do. Why didn't you go to them while I slept here?"

Peta rocked on his knees, knuckles ivory against the rough floorboards, face still down.

Durell continued: "You could have gone to the police, as any offended person might on finding that his property was being stolen."

Peta raised himself up, moved warily around Durell, tall, thin frame rippled with muscle.

Durell said: "I don't believe your father ever registered his claim. Something—or someone—kept him from doing that, otherwise the title would be clear and you could enforce it through the proper authorities. Who was it, Peta? Who did that to your father?"

Peta held a stubborn silence. The sunlight struck his irises from the side, and its radiance swarmed in their hateful green. A bottlefly buzzed and looped and sparkled through the white shafts of hot light. Durell saw confusion and bewilderment, and, in the knit brow beneath the shaggy cap of iridescent black hair, enough mistrust for a dozen men.

When Peta spoke, his voice was low and taut. "It was Mr. Eisler," he said.

"Calvin Eisler?" Durell was skeptical. "Why?"

"My father was not paroled from Devil's Island. He escaped and came here. He lived in the forest with my mother's people for many years and looked for gold and diamonds. What little he found, he traded away. Then I grew up. Mr. Eisler gave me a good job. He met my father and grubstaked him. When my father came back out of the jungle, he said he had found many diamonds. Mr. Eisler told him if he filed a claim, he would see that the police took him back to prison. My father had to sell his diamonds cheap to Mr. Eisler." Peta's chest heaved with anger.

Durell remembered that Devil's Island had been closed down years before. Escapees and *libres* who had broken their parole and fled French Guiana were living unmolested all over South America. No one really cared anymore. The French were glad to be rid of them— they could never return to their homeland. And authorities here were willing enough to accept them passively, considering the cruel hell-hole in which they had suffered. In most cases their fugitive status became a distant technicality—unless they fell into the web of someone such as Eisler.

He said, "If we find your father, I'll help him get the best legal advice. If he has a clean record, it's possible the French won't press the case, or that Guyana won't allow him to be extradited. . . ." He saw a blank look on Peta's face, drew a breath and simplified: "Good lawyers might make it so that your father never has to worry about the police again, Peta."

"Words." Peta grunted. "Just words to fool me."

"I want to help you."

"Mr. Eisler stole from my father. Now you want to do the same, that's all."

The boy's mind was numbed by suspicion, Durell judged. It listened only to its own thoughts. "I'm the only friend you have," Durell said.

"Such a friend I won't let out of my sight." Peta's eyes were murderous.

"I'll settle for that."

Durell scooped cartridges out of his pocket and replaced shells spent the night before with fresh ammunition.

"Come on," he said.

They went into the fiery green sunlight and turned north, toward the abandoned sawmill. The pace of the town had slowed as people napped through the steamy afternoon. As the congestion of buildings thinned, a scabby cur trotted after them, tongue lolling. Then it turned aside, and Durell saw no living creature behind. Far across the flaring Mazaruni the jungle was blue smoke that lay above its reflection. The street dwindled to a grassy path banked with heart-shaped caladiums and arums, and Durell walked without any show of hurry, Peta glistening and silent at his side. Below stretched a tongue of saffron beach, frilled with water-worn fruit, branches, leaves; drifts of red, purple and yellow blossoms; beans the size of a woman's handbag. The cayman seemed to have been exterminated here, hunted for hides and teeth.

"How will you sell my diamond if the police have it?" Peta asked.

"I'm not selling anything," Durell said.

"Then why go?"

"Maybe they will tell me how to find the Warakabra Tiger," Durell said.

He wondered what answers waited in the swaybacked old sawmill that loomed out of the jungle fringe ahead. There had been an elusive thread in Jan Browde's role, something unconvincing, a factor that warned the instincts without informing the processes of logic. . . .

They stopped before the rusting shed of the mill, and Durell's dark gaze surveyed the liane-bound trees that leaned toward him, the high mounds of sawdust that moldered under coverlets of creepers. His eyes turned toward the glare of the river, found it empty in the heat of the day, except for a huge raft of timber rounding a bend upstream.

The scream and rattle of insects frayed against Durell's nerves. A horde of blackbirds with hooked beaks jeered. The metal building emitted a solid layer of heat as Durell reached for the door. He steeled himself and stepped inside. A shaft of white light came through the door behind him and carried his shadow deep into the building. He stepped aside, and his shadow mingled with the gloom. Peta came in beside him, while he waited for his eyes to adjust from the blaze of the sun.

Then Peta said: "Nobody's here."

"Be still."

Durell listened. He heard no one, but had an indefinable awareness of another's presence. He unloosened his S&W and picked his way down the sloping dirt floor. The rear of the building was open and framed a molten shine that was the river. The water's reflection wove ribbons of light against the ceiling, wavered over rust-caked machinery that had been the headrig. The deepest roots of his mind, the seat of primitive emotions and mechanics of heartbeat, said something was terribly wrong, and he saw the same recognition in Peta's green eyes. But nothing looked wrong.

They paused beside a water-filled log pit at the river's edge. Rainbow-hued guppies and orange and silver characins mingled beneath the still surface. Durell lifted his gaze toward the river, where wavelets splintered the sun's rays. The log raft was closer now, and he saw a woodcutter, wife and children, dark, somnolent figures under a thatch awning. The river plashed and purled against the gate of the log pit.

The place was empty.

Durell was baffled and shook sweat from his face.

He heard the heat in his ears, the dim jangle of alarms in the recesses of his intelligence as he moved warily around the broken-down hulk of the log carriage.

Then the alarms screamed, and he heard the short suck of Peta's breath.

Otelo would never write again.

Chapter Twenty-one

Otelo Antunes' corpse was almost unrecognizable there in the sawdust with ants running over its flat, black eyes.

Peta's breathing quickened a bit, the wavelets' glare pulsing across his bare back, and he bent next to the body. Durell looked all around, then down. The man's neck had been broken, and the doughy mass of his crushed head lay at a bizarre angle to the line of his spine. His smart gray suit was ripped and tattered, his shirt front torn away completely. Lines of deep scratches were gouged across his face and chest. A savage combination of rips ended below the breastbone, as if made in a ferocious digging at the man's viscera, which had been disembowled and lay in bloated gray lumps and coils in the bloody dirt.

The youth's lips twisted distastefully, and he turned his face up to Durell. "It looks almost as if—"

"As if an animal had killed him," Durell supplied, and his jaw muscles stood out in ridges. "A big cat."

"The Warakabra Tiger!" Peta's eyes went glassy.

"Don't believe it," Durell said. He knew Peta worried

about his father and put a hand on his arm. "I've a hunch this is a trap, set especially for me. Too bad you stepped into it."

"I don't understand . . . "

"Nor I; not clearly." Durell's eyes swung around to the front of the building, and he added: "The trap isn't sprung, yet. Let's get out of here."

Then a bullhorn sounded: "This is the police. You in the building, come out peaceably!"

Swiftly, Durell holstered his pistol, stuffed his shoes into his trousers pockets, threw his jacket into the log pit to sink. "The river's the only way to go," he said and splashed through the log pit as shoals of tiny fish scattered like tossed gems.

Peta seemed held to the spot for an uncertain moment, then lunged after Durell.

"Head for the timber raft," Durell said, and clambered over the end wall of the log pit, dived and swam with urgent power.

The bullhorn demanded his obedience once more. He ignored it and hoped the building would shield him from view until he was out of pistol range. The water was tepid, as Peta matched him stroke for stroke. The raft of timber was still upstream, and Durell allowed the current to speed him on a tangent to intercept it. They were three or four hundred yards out before the police realized what had happened, and Durell heard the first flat crack of a gun. A bullet slapped the water yards away. Durell did not pause or dive, kept up a steady crawl, and the raft loomed larger.

More bullets spanked the water as the midstream current hastened Durell's pace. He glanced back, saw half a dozen police running and gesturing, and thought about the voice that had sounded through the bullhorn—it had been Inspector Sydney James'.

Bartica was out of James' bailiwick, so it was logical for Durell to assume that he had come here to entrap him—which implied that the inspector had been

124

tipped off about his meeting with the diamond pirates and might even be guilty of complicity in Otelo's murder.

Durell was ready to believe anything.

The raft loomed beside him; he reached out, clutched the rough bark of a huge log, and his shoulders cracked with strain as he pulled himself onto it. He straddled the log, gave Peta a hand up, and Peta flopped down beside him, water streaming from his hair.

The lumberman came running.

He made the machete in his hand obvious, as he said: "What are you doing on my raft, man?"

"Just hopping a ride. We'll be off in five minutes," Durell said.

The dark lumberman was a bowlegged runt, but muscle squirmed under his skin, and he looked willing to use the blade. "I saw them shoot at you. Get the hell off."

Durell scanned the riverbank, saw that the cops had vanished, probably running for a launch. The man's wife stood in the shade of the thatch shelter, cotton print dress sagging about her hips, two naked children peering from behind her skirts. Durell did not want to harm the man. He was relieved when Peta spoke.

"Where did your timber come from?" Peta asked.

"Up Issano way. Why?"

Peta's smile was pleasant. "You know Edmund Bannon? Stanley de Courcy?"

"Hey! You know Stanley?"

"Good friends," Peta replied.

"His concession's next to mine!" The woodcutter buried the edge of the machete in a log and held out his hand and grinned.

Durell felt the sun dig through his drying shirt. A gleaming dragonfly landed on the log, as the great strength of the river whispered about them. He saw the hill above Bartica clearly now.

He spoke to Peta. "Swim for that custard apple down there. The current will do most of your work."

"That's the place I showed you this morning."

"Yes. Dick's house is just up the slope."

They splashed ashore in the hot shade of the tree, and an iguana scurried into the river. Peta and the wood-cutter exchanged a wave as the raft glided past. Durell strode rapidly up a grassy slope, scattering water from hair and clothing, and stood before the box of weathered wood and rusted roofing that was Dick's outpost shack. Red brick pilings held it above flood level, and it had shuttered windows and a deep porch. The house was no different from a hundred others, except that the porch was empty of clutter, and rough boards had been nailed across the door. A notice tacked there said the house had been sealed by the police, and KEEP OUT.

"You did not kill that man. Why did you run?" Peta asked as he yanked at the boards.

"Why did you?" Durell said.

Peta eyed him narrowly, then gripped a board and heaved until his muscles lumped like stones.

"It's no use, Peta. We won't get them loose with our bare hands."

"We need a crowbar," Peta agreed.

Durell wondered where the police were. Sooner or later they would look for him here. "We've got to hurry," he said. "Maybe something is under the house."

They ran around to the side of the building. It had been sited on a slope, so that this side was some six feet off the ground. Durell thrashed through a fringe of weeds, hoping against the presence of bushmasters and coral snakes, the heat of the open sun an intolerable weight that burdened mind and body. Then the dank space beneath the house was cooler, floored in soft, red earth, all vegetation shaded out. Casual junk. A darting rat. Discolored bottles and remains of corroded tin cans. A pick head. Durell bent for it, abruptly realized the footprints beside it, raised puzzled eyes toward the floor.

A square cut outlined a trap door.

Peta met his gaze, shrugged.

Durell tested the door, found it unlocked and flicked his .38 from its holster. He hoped the water had not penetrated its cartridges. He put his cheek close to the warm boards and raised up slowly.

No one shot at him. There was no cry of alarm.

The room was dim behind its shuttered windows, smothered under the sun that hammered on its tin roof.

"What do you see?" Peta whispered.

"Nothing. Nobody."

They pulled themselves onto the floorboards, and Durell stood in the center of the room, gun hanging at his side. It was not what he had expected. There were no filing cabinets, no desk or working space. At one end was an old-fashioned water pump, its spout angled toward a sink of galvanized metal, kitchen cabinets of rough lumber, a small wood-burning stove for cooking, a simple dining table and pair of chairs. At the other end was the living area, an old bureau, a narrow iron cot, neatly made, under mosquito netting, a worn sofa and two sagging easy chairs.

Someone once had lived here comfortably, if simply, Durell thought, but not Dick—at least not for a long while. There was no food in the kitchen, no clothing in the bureau.

Durell conjectured that Dick's only use for the place had been for overnight stops, or—remembering Eisler's accusation—for meetings with the restive East Indians.

He rifled it, the closet, the chest of drawers, then the cabinet.

He was digging through knives and spoons and bottle lids when he found the wrinkled note. Written in a crabbed, rough hand, it read:

> Dick
>
> I got jonah to bring this with him to bartica. Told him how to get in your house. I am waiting here for you. I got another look at the dam. Sketch on other side shows where I figure weak points are. Should check them first.

It was signed, "Claude."

Durell flipped it over with trembling fingers and found a pencil drawing of a dam with X marks at the two wings and a third point labeled "turbine intake."

The sketch had only one meaning for Durell: explosives planted in the dam. It explained why Dick had attempted to inspect the structure, and what he was doing there when the Chinese apprehended him.

A breath-sucking dread crept over Durell, not for the dam or its keeper, Colonel Su, but for the life of every high official of Guyana.

They all would be atop that dam for its dedication tomorrow morning.

If Leon had his way, the peace of Guyana would be shattered—and Durell suspected that was only a prelude to a flood of revolution that would be unleashed to devastate the whole of South America.

His voice was tight as he spoke to Peta. "Your father is waiting for Dick to bring help, but we're the only ones who can help him now. Will you take me to his claim?"

Peta stared at the note.

"I will help my father," he said.

Chapter Twenty-two

Rick Kirby shoved the throttle forward, and the Cessna Skywagon bore up the river. Spray whirled in its propwash, pontoons bumped and thudded against bits of debris swept down from distant rain forests, and Durell hoped there were no logs in their path. Then the red and blue aircraft leaped from the water and bent a half-circle out of the azure sky, headed west into the sun, along the brassy track of the Mazaruni River. Widely spaced squall clouds trailed banners of rain across the endless jungle ahead, while behind, Bartica was a pile of children's blocks spilled onto a green rug, the horizon walled by damp haze.

Durell's backward glance showed relief that was only momentary. The next hours would bring a confrontation with Colonel Su, a dash to Claudius' claim and—hopefully—a decisive encounter with the Warakabra Tiger.

How it would go was only guesswork, speculation.

He could not know which way it would end.

Peta, an unwilling partner at best, plainly jealous of Ana and protective of his father and the claim, might undo all his efforts in the final test.

Durell had no choice but to rely on the somber youth and hope for the best.

The climb peaked as Rick throttled back and dug a black cigar from his shirt pocket.

The dam was on a tributary of the Mazaruni thirty miles west of Tumereng, in foothills of the Pakaraima Mountains, and Durell judged it would take about an hour to reach it. He looked at his wristwatch, guessed that darkness was likely to descend before Peta could guide him to the claim—but night could be an ally. Especially if you were outnumbered and outgunned.

The engine hummed as the hot air tossed the little aircraft, and the dimension of the ancient jungle, where time had no meaning, reached up and engulfed them. The minutes oozed by. Their progress seemed in inches, measured against the green monotony far below. The billowed trees were woven together like fabric down there below the wings of an eagle splashing the sun, and Durell thought of explorers and prospectors and wondered how they survived such savage wilderness.

"There she is. The lake." Rick pointed into the harsh sunrays, where Durell saw a golden slab of water. To his left the forest floor threw up mountain ramparts, and he might have glimpsed the haze-shrouded plateau of nine-thousand-foot Mount Roraima some eighty miles to the south. From his boyhood he remembered Sir Arthur Conan Doyle's book, *The Lost World,* inspired by tales of that jungled spire where Venezuela, Brazil and Guyana met.

Durell reached between the seats, added his .38 to the

other guns in his suitcase and turned to Rick. "Do you have a parachute?"

"What for?"

"Do you have one?"

Rick stared from behind the mask of his sunglasses. "Behind the back seat, but you'd be crazy to—"

"I'm not jumping." Durell told Peta to retrieve the chute, then harnessed it to the suitcase. He spoke to Rick. "I want to drop the suitcase before we reach the dam."

"You're the customer."

Durell hoped the Chinese would cooperate with him, but that would not be very likely if they found him armed. The weapons would be useful later, however, when he moved on Claudius' claim. The big diamond, Claudius' note, everything pointed to that claim or its vicinity as a staging area for the assault on the dam. If Claudius were not there now, Durell felt safe in assuming someone else would be.

The lake was a wrinkling metal that burned under the westerly sun.

Peta leaned forward, eyes squeezed against the brightness.

Durell said, "Are you oriented?"

Peta made no reply; his face revealed nothing.

Durell again regarded the vast, treacherous rain forest, considered the odds against him down there if not for Peta's knowledge and assistance. Worry burned in the core of his stomach.

Peta needed his help as well, and Durell told himself the kid was sensible enough to know that. He told himself to trust Peta, if only because their goals chanced to coincide. But he could not quite do so.

He turned to Rick. "Descend to three hundred feet. Take us around the south end, away from the dam."

Rick nodded, the cigar clamped under his mustache, pushed the aircraft into a shallow, banking glide, and the engine roar fell to a muttered whisper.

Durell struggled the suitcase and parachute onto his lap, unlatched his door. The wind puffed and whistled into the cabin. He kept his eyes on the lakeshore, but it was not easy to find landmarks down there. The forest all looked the same, down to the water's edge. He decided on the point of a ridge that formed one low wall of the lake valley, spoke to Rick, and the ridge glided closer, its point taking form with shaggy vegetation and tumbled rocks. The treetops showed little, if any, wind, and Durell counted on a relatively straight drop into the sultry stillness.

He jerked the ripcord, felt the chute restraints pop, smothered the silk against his chest and worked the suitcase out the door.

The chute unfurled as it went out and settled seconds later near the stony outcropping, some three miles from the dam.

He slammed the door shut. "All right," he said, "let's go see the Chinese."

The lake, still filling, sent glittering fingers up valleys, gullies, hollows, cutting off innumerable islands, its backwaters burdened with rafts of debris. To the west ran a narrow whip welt, a road built at enormous cost to bring equipment from Morawhanna on the coast, up the Kaituma River, then by railroad to the manganese mines at Matthew's Ridge.

The Chinese had spared no effort, no expense to construct their Latin American showpiece. In twenty years half a dozen similar dams would be completed, harnessing seasonal floods that rose twenty or thirty feet and generating power to open the interior and exploit its vast reserves of ore and timber.

But in a few hours—literally overnight, now—the destiny of Guyana could change—and that of the whole continent with it.

Durell knew a determination not to let that happen.

They skimmed down the lake. As they neared the dam, Durell made out a prefabricated village, apparently of workers' quarters, offices, shops and the like, bunched on raw earth at the water's edge. Durell glimpsed the fluttering banner of Guyana, a green field with a black-edged triangle superimposed on a yellow triangle. Beside it flew the five-starred red flag of the People's Republic of China.

Then they turned into the wind, drifted down, and the pontoons smacked the water.

"I hope you've got friends here," Rick said. "Those Chinks don't like people dropping in without an invitation."

The construction camp still was a quarter-mile away, when Durell felt something brush past, then saw Peta dive out the door.

"Where the hell's that kid going?" Rick yelled.

"I don't know," Durell said, dismayed.

"He must be crazy. We'd better go get him."

Rick started to turn the plane, but Durell touched his arm and shook his head, and said, "We have to let him go."

If they attempted to stop the youth, he would fight, and that would be the end of any help he might have given, Durell reasoned. He could not force Peta, could only hope he would have second thoughts, alone out there with the Warakabra Tiger.

He regarded his watch bleakly and thought about the ceremony atop the dam tomorrow morning.

He picked out two twin-engine amphibians tied up as they approached the dock. One was a Canadair that Rick identified as the Chinese company plane.

"Are you familiar with the other one?" Durell asked.

"Sure," Rick said. "The Grumman Goose belongs to a bigwig name of Calvin Eisler."

Chapter Twenty-three

"Sam, this is your last chance."

"You're pushing too hard, Ana."

"I—I know I'm interfering. . . . "

"Yes."

"But if you don't leave, something terrible will happen. I just feel it."

"You're playing Eisler's game."

"Just because we want the same thing, doesn't mean we have the same reasons."

"Not necessarily."

Ana's taffy brown eyes emphasized her anguish. Her boots and jungle khakis still were spotless, despite the previous night's travail. The spell of her slender femininity seemed to defy dirt and grime, Durell thought. She had rolled her black hair under the billow of a soft, visored cap and applied fresh makeup, a touch of delicate fragrance.

They had all waited on the wooden dock for Durell's aircraft to tie up—Ana and the squat threat that was Colonel Su Chung of the *Cheng pao k'o,* or Political Security Section, Black House, and Calvin Eisler, plus over a dozen armed Chinese and a sprinkling of curious Guyanese.

It seemed that he had been expected.

"How did you know I'd be here?" he asked.

"Just a hunch." She took a small step backward. "Sam—I don't like the way you're looking at me."

His expression did not change.

She blew a little breath. "All right, Sam. I admit it. I knew you'd be leaving Bartica, most likely by air, and I still wanted to be part of what you were doing, so—" her smile trembled "—I went to the seaplane base and found out who you had hired and asked him your destination."

Durell regarded Ana, then turned his eyes to the ominous Chinese, his thoughts on his objectives here. He must get the dam inspected for explosives, then push into the jungle and somehow find Claudius' claim.

It was bad enough that Peta had deserted him.

Now he had Ana to contend with.

Ana spoke to his angry silence, her voice low. "The

police are hunting you, Sam. They say you murdered Otelo Antunes."

"Somebody did."

"The police killed that East Indian you brought to my plantation last night—evidently Leon turned him over to them."

"They killed Ajit?"

"They claim he was escaping—they'll say you tried to escape, too."

"And you're going to help me?" Durell's voice was dry.

"I told you: Calvin and I will fly you to Timehri Airport, and you can board a plane for home. The police won't expect you there, after seeing you in Bartica earlier today. You've got a decent chance of getting away—before it's too late."

"What about Colonel Su? He would be delighted to see me arrested, the U.S. further embarrassed."

"It's all been worked out, Sam. He doesn't know about Otelo. All he wants is to keep you away from here. He has accepted Calvin's word as a national assemblyman to take you away and see that you don't come back."

"That's very tidy, Ana—except that I won't go."

"Sam—"

Durell shoved past her and approached Colonel Su and Eisler. Eisler's limp blond hair hung over one aristocratic eyebrow, and his blue eyes studied Durell as if he were a distasteful laboratory specimen. He said, "Well, Durell? I really don't know why I'm being so bighearted about this. Ana talked me into it, I suppose."

"Still trying to get me out of the country, aren't you, Cal."

"Now, look here—"

"Shut up."

For the first time Durell's eyes met Su's, and he saw that those bright, black slits were full to the brim with decades of hatred for the West, its decadence and undisciplined waste, its corrupting wealth and history of colonial oppression. Durell knew the lines by heart. He could almost hear Su speak them as he exchanged stares with the flat-nosed old revolutionary. Su might live in an era that was past, Durell thought, but nothing could change the fact that the colonel regarded him as the personification of everything he had been taught to fight and despise.

Out of Georgetown, the Chinese intelligence officer wore a blue Mao jacket. Only a pistol belt broke the simple line of his clothing, and the heel of his hand rested on the butt of a Tokarev identical to the one Dick had brought out of the jungle.

Su spoke to Eisler. "Mr. Durell refuses your kind offer. I see it by his face. Am I not correct, Mr. Durell?"

"Quite correct, Colonel Su. I came to help you save your dam."

Su's teeth winked a tiny smile. "But I do not see the threat—unless you brought that as well. Are you something new? A virus that cures itself? A rabid dog that bites only its own hindquarters?"

"Perhaps something new is what's needed—an American to protect you, since the Chinese seem incapable of defending themselves."

Color flared angrily on Su's cheeks, and he said: "I told you once to stay away from here. I could not have made myself clearer."

"And I would not have come, but necessity demanded it. Someone's going to blow up the dam. Look at this." Durell showed the sketch drawn by Claudius. "Explosives may be hidden at those points."

"Nonsense. This project is guarded day and night. Your late colleague found that out."

Durell spoke loudly, playing to the other Chinese so that Su could not afford to take a chance, even to save face. "If it happens, you can't say you weren't warned."

Contempt twisted Colonel Su's mouth as he snatched the sketch.

Durell hoped he could allay the man's suspicion somewhat, and said: "I have no wish to help the PRC, Colonel. It happens that our aims coincide, just as they did in Angola, against the Russians. You need stability to further your objectives—but if this dam goes up tomorrow, you can kiss it all off; there won't be any stability in South America for a long time."

Su's gaze responded uncertainly.

"Like it or not," Durell said, "we're on the same side."

Su thrust the sketch at an aide and spoke in Chinese: "Have the locations inspected immediately."

It took about fifteen minutes. Durell waited on the wooden pier, along with the others. The slanting sun spilled heat that was acid on his exposed face, and sweat trickled down his neck and darkened his shirt. Ana showed discomfort only in a dewy film above her small, provocative mouth. Her hands clasped and unclasped, eyes drifting from Durell to the Chinese to Eisler. She made no attempt at small talk, for which Durell was thankful. His lungs sucked at the heavy, humid air as he watched men scale down the face of the dam, suspended in slings, probing the monolithic structure for instruments of destruction. A troop of howler monkeys screamed in the distance, and the noise rebounded from the concrete rampart.

Durell's eyes moved darkly to the camp, built on rutted yellow earth torn from the primordial rain forest, then to the forest itself, a dense screen a hundred feet high, wattled with looping, flowered lianes. The parachute was not visible from here, but he could see the butt of the ridge where it lay. He was confident of reaching the weapons. After that, he did not know. He had counted on Peta more than he cared to admit.

The return of Su's aide broke his thoughts. The two Chinese spoke briefly in low tones, then Su turned to Durell. "It is as I suspected, Mr. Durell. Our search shows no sign of explosives." His malice was complacent.

Durell was baffled.

Colonel Su ordered Rick to return to Bartica, and said, "Your passenger will remain here."

The pilot's tongue rolled his dead cigar to a corner of his mouth. "Well, I don't know about that. Mr. Durell is a paying passenger. I take his instructions, not yours."

"You will do as you're told." Su slid the Tokarev from its holster, and the other Chinese made restless movements with their automatic weapons.

Ana said, "Sam, please—send Rick away."

"Better listen to her, old boy," Eisler said. "I will guarantee your safety." His lank hand grasped Durell's upper arm. He saw the danger in Durell's eyes and released his grip immediately.

"If you refuse to leave with Mr. Eisler," Su said, "you will be held until the proper authorities arrive to take you into custody. It would be foolish to allow you to leave by yourself; you would only find other ways to make trouble. The police ordered you out of the country, and I predicted you would not obey them. You conduct yourself like the international outlaw that you are."

Durell's voice went tight with urgency. "At least postpone the ceremony. Or move it from the dam down here to your camp."

"You have something in mind," Su snorted. "You wish to manipulate me through fear. The snake tells the sparrow its nest may fall from the branch, hoping it will sleep in the grass. I'm not such a fool."

Durell regarded the impenetrable hatred in Su's eyes, considered the possibilities. If the dam wasn't rigged for destruction, it still could happen. There were other means—underwater mines, mortars zeroed in on the weak points, even aerial bombardment. It had not been constructed with defense in mind.

It—and those atop it tomorrow—would be completely vulnerable.

He saw plainly that the Chinese would not help him; that he must do it all himself.

"Rick can leave," he said. "I'll take my chances in the jungle."

"How desperate you must be, Mr. Durell. But I see." Su's teeth winked a smile, the damp quills of his hair seemed to lie back. "Yes, I understand. You were dispatched here to prevent the success of our project in any way you could, as was Richard Boyer before you. Our presence in the Western Hemisphere threatens the interests of your imperialist masters much more than in Africa and Asia. The sharp point of our progress is aimed at the heart of your empire, now. It puts your prestige at a crisis. And you've failed in your mission to stop us. Perhaps you hope to flee to Venezuela or Brazil and escape the wrath of your capitalist bosses. I assure you, Mr. Durell: without provisions or weapons you will die out there."

"I said I'd take my chances."

"It would be most agreeable to rid myself of you with such certainty. As you well know, my bureau has had for many years a standing order pertaining to the, ah, correct disposition of your case."

"I know." Durell remembered the red tab on his dossier in the Black House in Peking.

Colonel Su's voice was laden with implacable enmity, as he said: "It would give me boundless pleasure to execute that order directly and personally, but the present circumstances preclude such satisfaction." He glanced at Ana and Eisler. "However, if you volunteer against the jungle . . . "

Everybody watched as he thought about it.

Durell was better equipped than most men to survive out there. He'd had jungle training in the Canal Zone and experience all over the world, including a trek across the Amazon Basin in search of the Zero Formula. Su would know of his background, Durell thought, but he also would be aware of the near impossibility of barehanded survival.

Su's eyes were sly. "You should know," he said, "that if you return to the camp perimeter, you might be shot. It would be unfortunate. An accident . . . "

"You don't have to spell it out," Durell said.

"Come." Su waved his pistol.

"No!" Ana's face went white beneath the visor of her cap, and she stepped in front of Durell. "Sam, you mustn't. It's sure death!"

"The choices are all used up, Ana," Durell said.

"Not for me—I'm going with you." She clung to him

like the damp heat and miasmic odors that rippled down invisibly from the forest wall.

"Ana! Get in our plane this minute!" Eisler bellowed. His eyes flickered with rage.

"Do what he says," Durell urged. "I don't have time to discuss it."

Ana did not raise her voice, but her tone was unequivocal. "I wanted to help," she said. "I'm in this to stay."

"You've played me for a fool," Eisler shouted. "This is the end for us, if you go."

Su chortled, "Ah, you westerners, with your romantic notions." He shrugged. "It's not my affair. Mr. Durell, Miss Morera. Come with me."

Ana placed her hand in Durell's as if it were a charm to take them both to safety. Durell was opposed to taking her, but dared not chance a squabble that would give Su time or reason for second thoughts.

A hundred dark eyes followed the small party across the rocky yellow ground toward the shadowed forest. The racket of engines sputtered from the lake. Durell looked back, saw Eisler's Grumman taxi away from the pier as Rick threw his cigar butt into the water and watched.

A crowd of rough-looking laborers in dirty working clothes drifted around the clot of Chinese as they ushered Durell and Ana to the jungle's edge. They were drawn by curiosity, glad for a taste of excitement, growing rowdy. Su's flat face showed worry—he could not abide disorder—and he suddenly fired into the air. A red and green macaw screamed harshly and flapped away as Su turned to Durell and Ana.

"If you have changed your minds, say so now," he said in a stern voice.

A pause.

"Very well." He grinned wickedly at Durell. "May fortune save her favors for one more worthy than you."

Durell pushed aside the first sheaf of leaves and spoke over his shoulder.

"I'm used to making my own luck, Colonel."

Chapter Twenty-four

Durell moved immediately through the sunlight-fed fringe of rank jungle and into the gloomy vault of the high forest. The going was easier here, but still slow and wearying among the endless columns of great buttressed trees. The slope of the valley punished ankles and thighs; fallen trees hulked across their path; decaying wood vented an odor of rotten teeth; ill-tempered spider monkeys pelted them with nuts and twigs. They fought their way past one obstacle after another, alert for tarantulas, scorpions, anacondas—a countless variety of things poisonous or predatory.

"Sam, let's rest," Ana gasped.

"Not yet."

"I've got to get my breath." She knelt against the soggy leaves and ferns, slapped at a kabaura fly that had raised a blood blister with its bite.

Durell yanked her up, regarded her with annoyed eyes, cursed under his breath. Her small figure was a reed that swayed in the gloom, her cap askew, an ebony tendril of hair swinging across the red flush of her cheek. Her breasts heaved as she struggled to breathe the sticky air. They had been going uphill, and it had been difficult, and Durell sympathized with her, but he would not stop until he reached the guns. He could not see the rocky knob where they had been dropped.

The noise of an airplane rose above the chatter of monkeys and greenheart birds and insects.

"What's the hurry, Sam?"

"I've got to find the Warakabra Tiger." Durell stepped off, and she followed.

"But there is no Warakabra Tiger," she said.

Durell spoke gently. "Why don't you go back to the dam? They'll let you."

"Even if there were such a thing, how would you find it out here in this awful wilderness?"

Durell's eyes were grim as they swung left and right. "I have a feeling," he said, "that it will find me."

Ana shivered and peered into the dusky growth that Durell recognized as a climax rain forest. It was dominated by immense, red-barked morabukea trees and even taller greenhearts with golden trunks, innumerable and ancient, enormous shafts aimed at a sky completely blotted out by leaves.

They strained on up the flank of the valley, and Ana spoke to Durell's back. "I'm already lost; it all looks alike. If you'd go back, Colonel Su would let you fly out."

"Don't talk nonsense."

Durell glanced over his shoulder. She looked very young and defenseless. He was worried about her, but there was nothing he could do.

"Did you kill Otelo, Sam?" Her words were thin and shaken by missteps on the rough earth.

"No."

"Then who did?"

"I'll find out."

Durell wiped sweat from his face, flicked it from his fingertips, looked back, beyond Ana. There were only specklings of butterflies, bees, mosquitos, flying ants. The trickle of seeping water was everywhere, the tattoo of falling husks, leaves, fruit.

They grunted and gasped, stumbled and fell, clawed their way up slippery ravines and over crumbling, spider-infested windfalls. The earth became more uneven, and large, mossy boulders appeared among the trees.

Then, out of breath, legs aching, Durell was surprised by open sunlight that showed a scramble of house-size boulders and realized that he had reached the rotting ironstone of the ridge. The parachute would be nearby. He pulled himself onto a boulder near the top of the scree. The rocky debris was intergrown with vines, ferns, banana-leaved heliconias that sparkled with vermillion.

The sky was open here and its glare hammered at his eyes as he looked down the hill, barely able to see over the treetops that were frothed here and there with suds-like masses of blossoms. The lake was out of sight. He could see nothing in the trees down below, turned his eyes to the point of the ridge, found a glossy snatch of white—the parachute.

At first, Durell thought the impact of the fall had sprung the suitcase open.

Then he saw Peta. The youth moved out of the bushy shadows with the big Browning pistol in his hand.

"I was counting on your help," Durell said.

"I wasn't waiting to help you," Peta replied.

Durell looked at the gun and then the youth's hooded eyes. He did not doubt that Peta had intended to shoot him. "Too bad Ana came along," he said. "You'll have to help her. It'll take both of us to keep her from the Warakabra Tiger."

Durell knelt to the suitcase, expertly snapped the AK's steel folding stock into place, shoved the ammunition clip home. Peta did not stop him.

The mosquitoes and kabaura flies seemed not to bother his bare chest and legs. His jade eyes swept to Ana, and she returned his stare uncertainly, her hauteur gone in this deep jungle where Peta was at ease. Their roles were reversed now, Durell thought: it was she who did not fit, her kind who must depend on his.

"I'm sorry about last night," she said.

Peta replied frankly. "I'm not."

"Then can we be friends?"

"Maybe."

Another voice drawled from the shadows. "Just one happy family."

Durell's head jerked up, and he saw Rick Kirby come out of the trees. Ana and Peta gave him shocked stares. He grinned from under his handlebar mustache, his eyes still hidden behind sunglasses. "I set old Becky down on the lake," he said. "She'll still be there when we need her."

"What are you doing here?" Durell asked.

"I figured you could use another hand when I saw those Chinks take off into the jungle after you."

Ana spoke through her fingers. "Sam, they've tricked us—they're going to catch us out here and murder us, where no one will ever know!"

"Calm down," Durell said. He kept his eyes on Rick. "How many?"

"A dozen, maybe more. They dispersed the laborers first. Guess they didn't want anybody to know."

It did not surprise Durell that Su had come after him, out here where all the rules were suspended, but that did not account for Rick's presence. "You have other reasons," he said.

Rick shrugged. "Well—more than one old porkknocker back in Bartica recognized Peta as Claudius Gibaudan's kid. I didn't think you were coming out here for a picnic. . . . "

"So you smell diamonds." Durell's voice was flat. "They're out of bounds; they belong to Peta and his father."

"Wait a minute. I'm offering to help you."

"You'll be paid for it when we return to civilization— combat mercenary, officer per diem: it's more than I make."

"Shit! Per diem!"

"Take it or leave it. There's no time to argue."

Rick brushed at a cloud of gnats. "How about we settle it when we get to the claim?"

"It's settled, as far as I'm concerned." Durell turned to Peta. "What do you think? We need all the help we can get."

"No."

"I flew spotters in Nam. Shot down twice and made it back through the lines both times," Rick said. "I'd be handy."

"No," Peta repeated.

"Yes," Durell said. He tossed the hammer-shrouded Colt to Rick, brushed sweat from his eyes, pressed a button in the suitcase. A thermite bomb planted in its lining burst into a white blaze that would destroy trans-

143

mitter and cipher materials. He spoke to Peta. "The smoke will draw the Chinese. Let's get out of here."

Peta hesitated. Durell knew what he was thinking, and said: "You don't stand a chance of helping your father without us—you're too smart to think otherwise."

Peta led off.

Chapter Twenty-five

Peta moved them more swiftly through the jungle, but there was no help for the treacherous clay that might suddenly loosen its hold on a pallet of leaves and send one sliding and rolling; the betrayal of a *tacouba,* a fallen log, that might twist and dash one into a stream; the strained nerves of constant vigilance against snakes and bugs and backlashing branches.

Piles of green dung signified that the youth had picked up the dim outline of a tapir trail. It wound cunningly around the worst obstructions, and the small party put more distance between them and the Chinese with every step. Ana's slight, pampered figure had unsuspected stamina, and Durell wondered if she had been as winded as she had seemed on that first mad dash away from the lakeshore.

He kept an anxious watch for the Chinese as the sun dipped lower and the false twilight of the forest deepened.

He called a rest on the bank of a dark stream that slithered over sunken leaves, and they sat on a crescent of sand at a wide bend, where blue flowers drifted down from a petraea vine and floated away. There Durell saw the first evidence of prospecting activity, old trenches, weed-grown piles of white quartz, tent posts and remains of a wooden batelle pan for washing gravel.

A prospector had tacked his notice on a tree, near

where Ana lay amid ferns and wild ginger. Painted in black on a flattened tin can, it read:

BASIL SAMPSON
Lic. No. 5520 A
Sept. 17, 1975

It was a relatively recent claim, Durell noted. If it had paid well enough to file, its owner should still be working it. But the decaying implements clearly said that it had been abandoned.

Rick removed his sunglasses, revealing assertive gray eyes, and dropped into one of the trenches. He scooped up a few handfuls of gravel, spread them on his palm and discarded them in eager succession. Then he called to Durell: "Hey, look at this," and held out two stones. They were small and irregular, but they definitely were raw diamonds.

Durell surveyed the undergrowth as parrots squawked and a large bumblebee fussed along the streambank. This was a paying claim: no one would have left it voluntarily. His cheeks tightened.

"Put them back," he said.

"Sure thing." Rick's tone was cynical. He stuck the diamonds into his pocket, grinned at Durell. "It isn't exactly stealing, old pardner. The owner won't have any use for them."

"You don't know that."

"Oh, yeah?" He hoisted himself from the trench with a grunt, strode to the clearing's edge, parted the thick foliage of purple-berried melastomes. His curled finger beckoned Durell.

Human bones lay scattered among red-tinged spikes and spears of congo cane. They found the skull a few feet away. The bones had a raw look, as if the flesh had not decomposed, but had been chewed away. To judge by the moldering boots and tattered clothing the man might have died as recently as a month ago, Durell thought. He gingerly probed for a wallet, found one, opened it.

Rick had been right.

This was Basil Sampson—or what was left of him.

Peta approached, and Rick said, "Spooky, huh, boy?"

Peta did not reply. He touched Durell's shoulder and waved for him to follow, and went around the edge of the clearing parting leaves and pointing to scarred tree boles. Some had the bark ripped off to the height of a man. Saplings had been torn in two or ripped from the earth.

"Warakabra Tiger did this," Peta intoned.

But Durell did not have to be told.

Fear seemed to draw the little group closer together in the blue-green dusk of the remnant clearing. The muggy air quivered to the echoing shouts of greenheart birds. The creek chuckled.

Ana spoke. "Let's go back, Sam, before it's too late. We don't have to face the Chinese—Rick will fly us out."

"You seem to believe there is a Warakabra Tiger now," Durell said.

She lowered her eyes dismally. "Yes."

"I told you I intended to find it."

"And end up like that?" She pointed to the bones, then swung around to Peta. "Don't take him any further," she pleaded. "If you have any feeling for me, you won't go another step."

Peta's eyes showed his confusion. Ana leaned against him, cheek on his shoulder, body trembling, and he looked amazed and slid his arms around her, hands awkward and loose. "Please, Peta," Ana said.

His gaze went to Durell.

Durell just watched.

Peta spoke to the upturned oval of Ana's face. "I will take you back to the dam," he said in a gentle voice.

"It isn't just me, you idiot!" She beat against his chest and broke away. Her voice rose with fury and frustration. "You'll all be killed. Don't you see?"

"Hey, doll," Rick said, "settle down. If that Warakabra Tiger is still around, you'll have its skin for a nice coat by tomorrow—maybe your pockets full of diamonds to boot." He turned puzzled eyes to Durell. "What the hell *is* the Warakabra Tiger, anyhow?"

"We'll know when we find it," Durell replied. He turned to Peta. "Well, son?"

Peta regarded Ana, then said: "We must do the business we came for."

A rush of breath came through Ana's frowning lips.

Durell smiled without humor. "You're learning," he said.

Suddenly there came a distant thrashing, the mutter of Chinese voices.

Everyone stood frozen.

Durell concluded he had timed it about right. "Let's move out," he said.

The tapir trail played out, the slope steepened and the forest floor turned corrugated and littered with blocks of stone. Each moment challenged everyone's patience, sapped their strength. The pace ground down as they slowed for Ana, who did not have the physical size and muscle to keep up, and they were reduced to crawling up ravines on hands and knees, plagued by *bêtes rouges* that sought to burrow into the skin, giant wasps and odorous muniri ants, two inches long, black and bristly. They had a sting that could disable a man for a week. The air turned fetid with the musk of white-lipped peccaries, and Peta motioned for silence and led them deftly around the unseen herd. They were feared for their concerted attacks and cutlass tusks, Peta said.

A brief but blinding downpour added to their misery. At first it only rattled against leaves a hundred feet or more above, but quickly it strengthened and tore through the cover and left them soaked and chilled in the gray gloom.

Durell began to sense they were being watched.

He saw no eyes in the dribbling, plashing shadows, no abrupt shiver of leaves to betray a presence. But something, from somewhere, pressed in on a level of awareness that was feral and instinctive.

He kept slogging along and did not mention it.

He noted that Peta was utterly stoic, while Rick cursed and slapped, and Ana shivered. It was obvious to Durell that the youth still mistrusted him, whether because of Ana or a continuing fear that Durell schemed to steal his father's claim. But Peta never mentioned the big diamond.

They broke free of the woods at the foot of another weather-rotted ironstone cliff, approached it through vine-clad boulders, regarded its pitted surface as the last light of day washed it with eerie green radiance.

Peta pointed toward a dark, low hole among many that riddled the precipice.

"My father showed me that place. It will be good for a rest."

Durell looked back at the savage woods that stretched away. He did not know how far they had outdistanced the Chinese.

"How close are we to the claim?" he asked.

"Half an hour."

"Can you find it at night?"

"I think. It will take longer."

"We will wait for dark in the cave," Durell said.

Ana started to say something—but her words were cut short by the most bloodcurdling sound Durell had ever heard. It began as an angry, low mix of caterwauling gibberish and increased in volume to an ear-piercing scream, a high ululation that rode over a monstrous gallery of snarls and roars, as if a great seam had been wrenched open and loosed every demon in hell. It seemed to have no fixed point of origin, came from the sky and the earth and bounced insanely from tree to hillock and mountain to valley, the embodiment of everything fearsome and cruel, filling the twilight, the ears, the heart.

It died away with reluctant mutterings and hissings.

"God Almighty," Rick breathed in awe.

Ana's fingers went to trembling lips. Peta and Durell exchanged stares, and Durell felt his scalp crawl.

"Let's get in the cave," he said.

Chapter Twenty-six

Claudius was dead.

He had been shot in the arm and chest, but somehow had managed to drag his enormous bulk out of the jungle and into the low cavern.

He had waited for Dick, and Dick had never come.

He was a massive man, lying there in the dusk, at least six-foot-six and three hundred pounds. Tangled cables of raisin-colored hair and beard snared his immense head, and he reminded Durell of some figure of fable, a giant or demigod brought low. He had pulled a grimy blanket half over him as he lay next to a dead fire. One hand extended outward, and an open leather pouch lay next to it, and diamonds speckled the dust and stuck to thick blood on his palm and fingers. He looked as if he might have died only moments before. Green eyes like Peta's seemed to glare defiance from beyond.

Ana made a small sound in her throat, averted her face.

Rick put a hand on her shoulder. She shook it off, and he shrugged, peered out the cave entrance at the gathering darkness. "No telling what's out there," he muttered.

Peta squatted beside the body of his father, lips thin and stern. "I'll go no further," he said.

"You scared, kid?" Rick said.

"I am too sad."

Ana spoke. "We should all turn back. Right now."

"We can't quit now," Durell said.

Peta stared at his father. "I should have been here to help him. Otherwise, what are sons good for?"

Durell thought about it and decided he had to keep

Peta going however he could. "Sons are good for vengeance," he said.

Durell held his breath hopefully, as Peta raised fiery green eyes to him. "You are right," Peta said. "First, I will bury my father."

"We can't take the time."

"I won't leave him for the animals."

"Then we'll start without you. Can you show me the trail?"

Peta took him outside. Dusk had thickened over the shaggy countryside. The colors of the sunset had vanished from the clouds, which were purple against a deep blue sky. A jaguar's roar bounded through the valleys.

"See the ridge?" Peta pointed toward a black prominence. "Keep on a line between here and there. You will go down the hill, near the edge of the lake. When you reach a broad stream on that line, you will be at the claim."

Durell and Rick helped Peta haul Claudius' immense form away from the cave, then went back inside to Ana, who hovered over a fire she had started. The flames cast a light back into the cave, where a rusty shovel and pick lay next to a few provisions. Durell saw Dick's useless old transmitter back there and concluded that he and Claudius must have used this cave as a base of operations. Something had driven them away from the claim. It would not be easy to calmly go down there to it, he thought, but that was what he intended doing. He turned questioning eyes on Ana.

"I'm staying here," she said.

"It might not be safe."

"It'll only be worse down below."

"What if we don't make it back?"

"The Chinese will find me. Don't you think?"

"Most likely," Durell said. He shifted the AK in his hands. "Don't try to hold Peta back. We may still need him."

"I won't."

The firelight trembled against Ana's strained face,

dabbed at the golden swell of a breast beneath her partly unbuttoned blouse. She was scratched and bruised and muddied, like the rest of them, and a thin web of dark hair hung from under her cap, veiling an eye that reflected the firelight like a brass andiron. She had really tried, he thought, but it was better now that she go no further. He wished he could stop here, too. He was bone-weary, but a rest of any length was out of the question. Tomorrow the dam would be blasted; blood would begin to flow in a torrent to match the Mazaruni. He took a deep breath, aware of the musty smell of the cave, started to turn away.

"You could wait for daylight," she said.

"That will be too late."

"You will be killed, Sam. All of you." Her eyes were hot and dry, and her voice shook slightly. "Oh, don't give me that dark, competent look. No one thinks he will die."

"I don't have any illusions—"

Ana put her fingertips against his lips, and her sad, mysterious gaze held him a moment longer. Then she kissed him, hard, her lips damp and yielding as mellowed berries. There was something of dread and something of anger in the touch of her avid mouth, and then Durell broke free, slung the AK over his shoulder.

"Let's go," he said to Rick.

"I'm ready, pardner."

"Good-bye," Ana called, as they moved silently into the night.

Her voice was small and hollow out here, where Peta labored a grave into the tough soil down by the treeline some fifty yards below.

It was a strange voice, Durell thought.

The jaguar roared again, and its call rapped across the jungled ridges. The stars were out now, angry and swarming as if they had come up from the jungle. Their light made billowy curds of the massed tree crowns, and Durell thought how the air beneath those branches would be locked in darkness.

"Wonder where those Chinks are," Rick said.

"They can't be far," Durell said. The muscles in his jaw tightened, and he picked his way with slow care down the mossy scree, eyes on the distant ridge. They approached Peta, and Durell saw the milky light slide back and forth over his back as the youth worked with a pick beside the grotesque sprawl of his father's corpse.

"Hurry to catch up," Durell called.

Peta paused, back bent over the grave, and raised expressionless eyes toward the two men.

Then they merged with the trees.

A murmur of leaves was all that told Durell of Rick's presence at his heels. Their progress was agonizingly slow and halting. The air was rotten, suffocating. It fluttered and buzzed, black on black. Durell craned his neck up, and it was the same as if he'd looked at a hole in the ground. He moved like a ghost, willing his destination and approaching it implacably, as if without need of sight or touch, the imaginary line to the invisible ridge etched in his mind.

Rick spoke from behind. "I'd just as soon go back and keep that pretty gal company."

"Go ahead."

"You'd like to get rid of me, wouldn't you."

"If I wanted that, you wouldn't be here. You'll earn your pay."

"I must be crazy, but I'll stick with you." Rick hesitated, then said, "Do you think we'll run across that Warakabra Tiger?"

"If we're lucky—or unlucky, depending on how you look at it," Durell said.

He continued to work his way down among the buttressed giants, listening for the sound of the stream that Peta had described. The jungle was loud with a ragged chorus of chirps and whines and clicks. If anything, insects swarmed more densely than they had during the day, but now you couldn't see them. You couldn't see anything. Durell put his trust in his instincts to keep him on course, but he might as well have been blindfolded.

He told himself that it would do to intersect the stream anywhere; then they could follow its banks to the claim.

Abruptly he was aware of a stealthy pad of feet—off to one side. It was the kind of thing that came slowly upon the recognition.

He did not know how long they had been followed.

He moved on, and the crackling brush kept pace.

There was no indication from Rick that he had heard it. Durell unslung his AK, flicked off the safety, tried to suppress his heavy breathing as he jarred and lurched along. The memory of Basil Sampson's scattered bones burned across his mind; the nightmare scream that had shaken the earth and heavens.

A taste of iron came into his mouth, and he conquered a swirl of panic, came to a halt. Rick bumped into him, muttered an oath, a question.

"Quiet!" Durell hissed.

A few footpads rustled from the undergrowth, then went silent. The sounds had come from *both* sides of them.

Durell was aware that his hands were sopping where they held the AK. He pulled Rick down to a crouch, and whispered, "We've got company."

Rick's voice came through the gloom. Durell could not see his face. "How much farther to the claim?" Rick said.

"I don't know. Whoever is out there won't wait that long."

"Whoever? Or *what*ever?"

Durell made no reply, listened for a long moment. He moved his eyes, but nothing changed. He became aware that his teeth pinched his lower lip, loosened his jaw. Something scuttered along a branch, high above. Toads and insects mingled a raucous noise. The sodden air was still, laden with the scent of peat, humus, sap.

Finally, he said, "Come on."

A few paces and the rustle of leaves sprang up on either side of them again.

Then there was dim starlight, seen through a lacy

screen of fronds and branches, and they came to a long, straight swath clear of trees and underbrush. Rick started to cross it, and Durell held him back.

"We'll be sitting ducks out there," Durell said.

"So? What do you suggest?"

"Turn the tables—we'll have to take them."

Rick's swallow made a thick sound in the night. "Reckon I'm game if you are," he said.

"You go left; I'll go right," Durell whispered.

The leaden flakes of nightglow might have been painted on a backdrop for all the light they shed down here. Durell crawled through deep ferns and rotting wood, the AK slung under his chest, steadied by a hand. He paused, listened, heard nothing, then went on, inch by inch, his breath light and regular. The air had cooled, and his damp shirt was a chill plaster against his shoulders. In the back of his mind was the dread of a sudden scorpion or tarantula where he placed hands and knees. Every sense was alert, concentrated on the darkness around him.

He thought he heard something a few yards to his left, turned that way—then, all at once, he heard the smack of Rick's pistol, and something slammed into his back, knocking him onto his belly, and he jerked his face around with grit in his mouth.

From all around came that tremendous, paralyzing roar.

Chapter Twenty-seven

The roar turned to a mocking, highly amplified voice, and Durell was aware of knees in his back, a garrote around his throat, as it said:

"Very good, Senor Durell—but futile, I'm afraid. We have observed all your movements through infrared scanners."

Durell felt dizzy as the heavy cord cut into his breath, was dimly aware that someone had unslung his rifle. There must have been three men on his back and others around him. He did not struggle. It would have been suicide to resist. He was surprised that they had not killed him outright.

The voice had been that of Leon Perez.

Leon spoke again: "Are you quite content now? You did make it almost to your destination—"

"Go to hell," Durell said through choked breathing.

Leon laughed, and the sound of his sinister mirth clapped through the darkened valleys, just as the insane roar had earlier. "Ah, you're a man of one mind—a professional to the end. Perhaps we will postpone that end briefly. My men will bring you and your unfortunate friend to me."

An electric torch exploded against Durell's face, and he saw in its peripheral radiance half a dozen men in combat fatigues that had been printed with tigerlike stripes. Heavy jungle knives and ammunition clips were on their belts, and their AK 47s formed a semicircle of muzzles aimed at his body.

The man holding the flashlight said, "Come with us."

They took them to the line cleared through the forest and followed it down the slope. Durell decided the swatch had been cleared as a last barrier against anyone hardy enough to intrude after the electronic screams and mangled trees and mutilated bodies he might encounter on the way. It was doubtlessly under constant observation. He thought he saw the gleam of the lake in the near distance as the path rose over a low prominence, and guessed that the claim must lie not far from its backwaters. A few moments later they crossed into the forest and followed a narrow trail down to a clearing beside a wide, sluggish stream. The stream intersected numerous ditches that uncovered the diamond-rich gravel of former beds.

Leon had no reason to fear chance discovery, buried here in the heart of this vast wilderness, shielded by electronic surveillance, the large clearing amply lighted with kerosene lanterns. A thick blind of rank vegetation that fenced the clearing's boundaries contained their yellow glow.

The military primness and conformity of the thatch huts, the geometric paths of gravel and split logs struck Durell. The impression of an army encampment was reinforced by disciplined rows of shovels, axes and other implements beneath a shaggy-roofed lean-to.

They were shown into one of the huts, where Leon Perez waited.

His flame-whorled face was impossible to read, but there was satisfaction in the mad blackness of his eyes as he watched them from a canvas camp chair, booted feet on a table of rough lumber. The table was stacked with black-boxed electronic equipment, transmitter and receiver, infrared viewing screens, amplifier to carry Leon's voice or the taped screams of the Warakabra Tiger to speakers hidden in trees all over the area. Leon's Russian-made 9mm Stechkin machine pistol lay on the table. Durell recognized it from the night before.

"We should have brought you in sooner," Leon said, "but our little game was amusing for awhile, don't you think?"

"So Havana dreamed up the Warakabra Tiger," Durell said.

"The legend is ancient; we merely employed it. But how did you know our nationality?"

"An educated guess," Durell said. "Soviet weapons; Cuba's proximity and history of trying to export revolution in South America."

Leon's breath made a sound between his teeth, and he let a moment pass before speaking. "This time we will succeed, and the capitalistic enemies of the people will be swept away with the fury of a thousand tigers." He calmed his voice and said, "We have laid the groundwork with care. We are supplied regularly by submarine, as I believe you found out on the *Peerless*. We employ the wreck as a transfer point, and the men and provisions are flown here by amphibian."

"You run the operation from Ana's plantation?"

"It was convenient. Of course, I dare not chance that after last night." His eyes studied Rick for a moment, then dismissed him, and his fingers slid idly over the barrel of the Stechkin.

"And the diamonds are smuggled out in the sub," Durell said.

"For the benefit of world revolution," Leon replied, his tone smug. "Already the funds help pay for maintenance of our Cuban comrades in Angola, as well as make possible preparations for similar ventures elsewhere."

Durell regarded his eyes, aware again of that spark of vague familiarity, a fleeting thing that was gone in an instant.

Leon was saying, "At last we have within our grasp a foothold from which our revolution can liberate the peoples of South America. Tomorrow the highest officials of Guyana will be assassinated—"

"When the dam is blown?"

"Yes, and, given the current racial climate here—plus our own propaganda—the East Indian element will be blamed."

"Even though they had no part in it."

Leon nodded. "We could hardly entrust them with our plans in advance, could we. Nevertheless, they most certainly will be victims of a wave of mass repression. Then we will rally their resistance and secretly supply them with arms. A civil war will ensue. Who then will be capable of saying which side constitutes the legitimate government? Will it be the ruling blacks—who now hold de facto power—or the East Indians, who constitute a majority of the population?"

Leon paused, as if expecting an answer, but Durell just watched him. He had no inclination to debate the topic

157

—that was the sort of thing he left up to the diplomats with their Byzantine minds and preciosity of words.

Leon went on. "The East Indians will be most thankful to us for coming to their aid. They will form a government and call on the socialist states of the world for overt assistance, just as the Angolans did—and the U.S. can hardly afford to oppose us without suffering the condemnation of the rest of the world. Out of the destruction will emerge a new addition to the socialist camp."

Leon gestured disparagingly at the electronic equipment beside him, and added, "Then there will be no need for this silly game. Diamonds all over Guyana will be extracted openly for the further liberation of the continent."

"How much of this did Richard Boyer learn? He was your prisoner, wasn't he?"

"Senor Gibaudan led him right into our hands—unintentionally, of course. We had suspected that the old man was hiding in the vicinity. Somehow Boyer contacted him, and they came here to reconnoiter our position."

"What about the news story?" Durell asked. He saw his breath in the cool, humid air.

Leon spoke freely, preening his ego. "We had reason before Senor Boyer turned up here to believe he was onto our scheme. Nothing moves without leaving a trail, and the East Indians at Miss Morera's plantation may have dropped hints of our activities on the river—Boyer had wormed his way into their confidence. He had to be eliminated, but only after the most elaborate preparations had been made to ensure that the act would not be traced to us, but would be blamed on his East Indian friends. Revealing him publicly as an operative of your hated agency was a stroke of genius, don't you think?"

"But the story broke while he was in the jungle," Durell said.

"Yes, and Boyer was shot when he stumbled across our men on the *Peerless*, after escaping from us here—but the end result was the same, wasn't it?" Leon's gaze sharpened. "And tomorrow—"

"Tomorrow your whole plot goes down the drain. Whoever is helping you at the dam has failed to plant explosives on it. Security is too tight. It's impossible."

Leon might have smiled, the rubbery mask of his face wrinkling up around the simmering black eyes. "I need no help," he said. "It will be done. In fact, you will see—or at least hear it. That is why it pleases me to spare you temporarily, so that I may enjoy your anguish as you experience the complete ruin of your mission. Then will be time enough to dispose of you and your friend."

Rick spoke up. "Hey, old buddy, I don't know anything about this business. Hell, I was just going prospecting with this guy."

Leon's eyes glittered at Durell. "Your friend has a sense of humor."

"He's telling the truth—after a fashion," Durell said.

Leon turned to Rick, and said, "Then there is really no point in waiting to be rid of *you,* is there?"

Grapes of sweat hung from Rick's blond eyebrows, and his lips moved, but no sound came out. He looked at Durell with wide, gray eyes.

Durell's voice was calm. "Maybe your plans aren't one hundred percent sure," he told Leon. "They never are in our business; there's always the element of risk, the chance, however remote, that something will go wrong. Rick happens to be a pilot, and his plane is parked on the lakeshore not far from here if you go straight across the water. Maybe you'd like to keep Rick around—just in case you need him."

Leon thought about it for a moment. Insects clattered against the lantern chimneys. Mosquitoes sang around Durell's ears. Tiny crickets hopped and chirped on the earthen floor. The cooling hours of night had thickened the scent of the looming forest, and Durell briefly considered its tangled depths, wondered about Peta, who must be out there somewhere—unless he had turned back after all.

Rick's eyes shifted nervously from him to Leon.

Finally, Leon said, "Have you proof of this?"

"I've got a pilot's license," Rick blurted and eagerly

tossed his wallet onto the table. "And here are the keys to my plane." He yanked the key ring from his pocket with a metallic rattle.

"Very well," Leon said. "An intelligent suggestion, Senor Durell." He stood up and grasped the Stechkin casually, sure of his competence. "You will be held under close guard, and you will be shot on the slightest provocation. Is that clear?"

He ordered the guards to take them.

Durell glanced at his watch as they were marched across the orderly clearing. In a few hours the dam would go, and the peace of a continent.

He was powerless to prevent it.

Chapter Twenty-eight

"We're in one hell of a mess now," Rick said. "We've got to get out of this place."

He stared through the rough saplings that barred the walls and roof of their small prison. It was a six-by-six cage, out in the open where the sun would fry them in half a day—but they did not have to worry about that, Durell thought. The hour of the dedication had been set for the cool of the morning, and everything would be over long before noon, if Leon had his way.

Rick's tone was incredulous, as he said: "That spic was going to shoot me on the spot, until you spoke up."

"He still will," Durell said.

"Yeah? What if he runs into trouble tomorrow?"

"Then you can fly him out—and he can shoot you somewhere else." Durell scrutinized the dirt floor, killed a couple of umbrella ants and sat down wearily.

"I'd bet we could take this thing apart with a little effort," Rick said. He yanked at the vine lashings, and their guard leveled his rifle at him and made a hostile, shoving motion. Rick stepped back from the bars, helpless anger wavering in his eyes.

"I wonder where that kid is," he said. "Bet he high-tailed it."

"I have a hunch he's out there, somewhere." Durell rubbed a sore thigh muscle and watched the guard.

"I guess he's no good to us anyhow. What could he do?" Rick sank down beside Durell, and said in a dismal voice: "I'm not scared of dying; I just hate the idea of sitting here waiting for it."

"Look," Durell whispered. He slid a hand behind him and grasped one of the bars and lifted the cage an inch off the ground.

Rick's eyes widened. "Well, I'll be damned." He grinned. "When?"

Durell kept his eyes on the guard, some fifteen paces away. "I don't know yet," he said. "There's nothing to do but wait."

"Guess you're right," Rick whispered. "Reckon we couldn't run far with a bucketful of slugs in us." He leaned against the bars and fixed his eyes on the guard, as if willing him to vanish.

But the guard kept a stubborn watch on them, his automatic rifle cradled in his arms.

An hour passed. The guard might have been carved from stone for all that his hooded eyes strayed from the men in the cage. Lights that shone through flimsy thatch walls of the lodges went out, one by one. From somewhere came the low voices of men, the scrunch of shovels and rattle of gravel against sieves, and Durell realized that the rape of the rich claim was progressing on three shifts.

Another hour went by. Durell thought of Ana back in that chill mountain cave and wondered if she had kept her word not to interfere with Peta. She might have prevailed on him to stay with her.

He put the thought out of his mind as his eye caught activity at the far end of the encampment. A squad of Cuban soldiers in their tiger-striped uniforms and heavily armed strode single file up the hill and into the jungle.

"Where do you think they're going at this time of night?" Rick asked.

Durell's voice went taut. "Someone must have stumbled into their surveillance network."

"Peta?"

Durell felt his stomach lurch. They would not trouble to take the youth prisoner—they would make another of their examples of him, leave his mutilated body to frighten away the next intruder.

The two men stared at each other, then both turned brooding eyes back at their guard.

Fifteen minutes, perhaps half an hour elapsed, and shouts came out of the gloom, followed by the rattle of automatic weapons, two bursts in rapid succession that cracked back and forth among the hills. Long minutes passed, and nothing else happened.

The soldiers did not return.

Rick nodded, caught himself, crossed his arms over drawn-up knees, kept sleepless eyes fixed on the guard.

A man came from one of the huts and made a circuit of the camp, extinguishing lamps until only two or three were left burning. Huge moths fluttered around them, hopelessly dazed by their attraction. The shadows of the bars, thin in the low light, fell across Durell and the dirt floor and reached out toward the guard. The forest made sounds of grief with its rasping, whining breath, its lost wails and shrieks. The stars spoke of cold eternity.

Durell considered the dam, glanced at his watch, realized how, shortly, people in Bartica would rise from comfortable beds to come here and be blown to bits. An overwhelming sense of urgency flooded through him, but he somehow found the discipline to contain it. He told himself that he must be patient.

And another hour passed.

The first guard was relieved by a second.

He felt despair.

The air had become very still, filled with thin jungle vapor, and a fur of mist lay over the wide, sluggish stream. The world seemed to hold its breath. Speckles of dew gleamed on Durell's clothing. Rick had surrendered to fitful slumber and shivered and muttered. For hours now Durell had sat unmoving. One guard succeeded another, and he had watched through slitted eyes, legs drawn up, chin resting on his knees. Through all those interminable minutes he had waited and hoped, senses stalking a turned back, a nodding head.

But the guards were alert and disciplined; the moment had not come.

And then it happened.

Durell's thoughts had drifted to that vague familiarity in Leon's eyes, and he studied the man's image on his mind even as his gaze monitored the guard. The wild pigeons might have burst from the forest first, or maybe he was startled by a sudden parting of banana and palm leaves at the clearing's edge—in memory the two things would merge. The next sight was what etched itself vividly into his brain.

The whip-form of Peta Gibaudan broke from the jungle, lips drawn back, face twisted with fury. The long whoop that vented from his chest said death, and the cutlass in his hands said first come, first served.

The youth's beastlike charge stunned Durell. He watched what happened over the next three seconds with a clarity unclouded by thought or reaction.

Peta's green eyes found the guard, and he twisted toward him with demented rage. The guard was quick, but not quick enough as he swung around from the waist and brought the AK muzzle toward the figure that hurtled at him. The cutlass made a silken yellow arc high above the guard's head, and the AK's barrel staggered up with a burp of panic, coughed thin smoke. The cutlass hissed, disappeared, and Durell's eyes found its point gleaming in a fountain of blood between the guard's shoulder blades, lodged there after cleaving from the junction of neck and clavicle through the spine.

Durell hurled the cage onto its side, ran for the AK.

"Where's Ana?" Peta cried and whipped the big Browning from his waistband.

Durell paused with a stare. "Don't you know?"

Peta's head made a sweeping gesture at the camp. "They got her."

Durell scooped the assault rifle from the dust, recovered a belt of clips that dripped with gore, tossed a couple of the guard's hand grenades to Rick, who moved toward the jungle.

The shocked silence of the camp gave way to sharp voices within the huts. A face looked out, and Durell squeezed short bursts through the flimsy walls, heard screams. He aimed at the next hut and the next, telling himself he could not afford to worry if Ana was in there somewhere where dust and splinters and lead flew. Shouts of terror and pain mingled with the racket of frightened birds.

"Let's get the hell out of here," he yelled.

"I came to save Miss Morera," Peta said, his face stubborn.

"She'll have to take her chances for now. Save yourself."

Durell fired a last burst at the huts, and they ran into the jungle.

The pursuit was swift and relentless.

Durell did not know how many men were after them, or how many parties they had split into. Clearly Leon had thrown every available man into the hunt, and they knew the topography stone by stone, tree by tree.

Durell first tried for the cliff where they had found Claudius, but was cut off in a brief and fierce fire fight before making a hundred yards in the overpowering darkness. There was a second blind encounter when he took a different direction, and it seemed the Cubans knew every move he made. Then he remembered the infrared spotters and cursed himself for not having tossed a grenade into the control center. As it was, they exposed themselves to instant death every time they stepped from behind a tree or boulder.

"So what do we do?" Rick whispered as they hunched in a narrow ravine.

"Backtrack," Durell replied. "Stay on your belly and follow me down to the edge of the camp."

"We will get Miss Morera this time," Peta whispered. "I saw the men take her from the cave. I—I hid."

"It's all right, Peta. You finally came."

"They must have eyes like cats to see through the dark. They nearly got me as I came down to the claim."

"I heard the shots," Durell said. He started crawling.

"What do you think they've done with her?"

Durell glanced toward the sound of Peta's voice, back there in the black air. "I can't say—but Ana's at the bottom of the list, son. Leon must be stopped before anything else," he said in a grave voice.

Fifteen minutes of slithering on sore elbows and knees, and they arrived at the fringe of the camp. Leon's men made little effort at silence, sure of Durell's limited vision, and their superiority in numbers and firepower. Their shouts echoed all around.

Durell pushed a bit closer to the camp, until he found himself scrambling over a springy, crackly mass that was only part of the enormous amount of brush and trees cleared by the Cubans for their encampment.

"We can't just sit here," Rick said, his tone edgy.

"Give me your lighter," Durell said.

He felt Rick's fingers, cold and damp, as they placed the lighter in his palm. He sparked a flame and thrust the lighter down through the branches and twigs and wet leaves and fronds to the dry rubbish beneath. The brush smoldered and stank for a long moment, then exploded into blaze. Sparks spun up through the foliage, and the stems and bark of small plants browned, spewed resinous flame.

The heat became intense.

The flames spread.

Durell hurried on down the border of the clearing, started more fires in dead brush left by the efficient Cubans.

By now men both in and out of the camp were in turmoil, their voices alarmed as they rushed about like distressed ants in the flash and glow of the conflagration. Guns racketed, and slugs pattered through the thick leaves around Durell.

Peta raised the Browning, and Durell slapped it down. "They don't know where we are—they're just shooting at the fire, hoping to catch us. Don't give us away."

Rick turned a scorched face away from the blaze and spoke to Durell. "You were pretty smart—this heat will blind the infrared sensors."

"The fire will help us in more ways than one," Durell said, and he gathered himself to dash away from the flames.

"How's that?" Rick said.

Durell had to lift his voice to be heard over the roar and sputter behind them. "Let's just get out of here for now," he said and scurried away.

A minute later he glanced back to see an immense greenheart make a towering candle against the night. White sparks showered into the crowns of adjacent trees, and a sloth fell a hundred feet like a fiery, screaming bomb. The fire billowed from tree to tree, its front broadening in a silken tide. Smoke drifted through the air, stifling the lungs.

"It's coming up the slope after us," Peta observed.

"Then keep your ass moving!" Rick shouted.

Durell's grim eyes scanned the forest quickly, but picked out no men among the writhing, mangled shadows. They could be down by the camp, or up ahead. They might be anywhere, he thought.

They jumped to their feet and ran, zigging and zagging through the orange lucency that jittered and shivered eerily under the forest roof. Vague forms of panic-stricken animals, capybaras, labbas, anteaters, scampered past the corners of Durell's eyes. He hoped the cleared swath they had encountered on their way here would serve as a firebreak, angled toward it, coughing now as the acrid smoke stung eyes and lungs. His tongue was dry as felt against the roof of his mouth, his guts knotted with alarm.

The racing sheet of flame thundered like doom as they

rushed into the cleared stretch, and Durell glimpsed the nude dawn straining above the eastern horizon.

Suddenly the crackling roar was that of guns, and Durell realized an instant too late that Leon had waited in ambush here to cut them down as they fled the blaze. He dived and, in midair, saw something small and dark bounce a few yards to his right.

"Grenade!" he yelled.

Then there was a blinding light. . . .

Chapter Twenty-nine

Durell willed himself to see.

The air was bright with smoke, and his senses recoiled from its stench. A sputter and hiss of dying embers came through the throbbing in his skull.

Dim black forms.

Great naked shafts against a sapphire sky.

His eyes fluttered, closed against the glare. It was as meaningless to him as a dream or the rush of alien land beyond a window. He could not think about it as he lay there in the hot sun and prickly stubble. He felt his throat move, heard a groan, kept his eyes closed.

It might have been a second later, or an hour, when a voice said, "Mr. Durell?"

Violent memories abruptly flooded his mind—the terror of the forest fire; the hand grenade. The Cubans . . .

He reasoned there was no point in prolonging it and opened his eyes. The broad, shaggy-haired form that leaned over him was Colonel Su Chung. His narrow eyes widened slightly and briefly at Durell's gaze. He made no move with the Tokarev pistol that hung loosely in his hand.

"So you finally made it," Durell said.

"Thanks only to the fire."

"I hoped you'd see it. The Cubans. . . ? "

"They put up a spirited fight, but their position was tactically indefensible. We came upon their rear." Su's eyes slid to the ground a few feet away. "Your friend was not so lucky," he said.

Durell shook the fuzz from his brain, raised himself on tentative elbows, noted that he seemed to have escaped serious injury.

The still form of Rick Kirby, lying beneath Su's gaze, told him why. The pilot's body had soaked up the grenade's shrapnel—only the concussion had found Durell. He crawled over, turned Rick's face out of the dust. The man was dead.

"I believe I owe you an apology," Su said in a harsh manner.

"Forget it. Did you find the woman?" He rubbed his eyes and wished for order in his groggy mind.

"She has been transported back to the dam. I sent a runner by the lakeshore to bring a boat."

Durell stood up, took a deep breath, looked around, abruptly tensed. "Where's the boy?" he asked.

"What boy?"

"Peta Gibaudan." He made a rough sound. "Never mind. Did you bag Leon Perez?"

"There were few prisoners. The Cubans were fanatics."

"His face is scarred. You'd remember him."

"No one like that," Su said.

Durell twisted toward the leaden shine of the island-studded lake. The sun was high and blazing. No sounds of life came from the forest. He looked down the long clearing, and urgency sharpened his voice. "Has your boat returned?"

"Yes, with kerosene to burn the bodies." Su's face showed puzzlement.

Durell glanced at his watch, and alarm grabbed at his throat—it was fifteen minutes until the time for the ceremony, when the heart and core of Guyanese official-dom would be atop the doomed structure. It was too late to get them to safety, and Leon was still at large.

Durell's nerves were taut, humming wires as he rummaged through the pockets of the dead pilot and brought out the keys to the Cessna.

"Something troubles you," Colonel Su said, "but surely there is no longer cause for alarm."

"There's every cause, colonel. Is your pilot here with you?"

"Yes. I brought every available man, but—"

"Let's get him," Durell said.

"Take her lower," Durell said and peered intently from the window of Rick's floatplane. He had saved precious minutes by going to the Cessna, moored some distance down the lake, instead of the Chinese aircraft by the dam. Still, it might not have been enough, he thought. This was his second sweep around the lake beside the obedient Chinese pilot, and the minutes ticked perilously away as he surveyed the watery chaos. The lake had invaded countless forested gullies, cut off hundreds of islets, uprooted rafts of liane-tangled trees. The burned section of forest was a ragged swatch of slate gray halfway up a low hill at the far end of the lake.

The small plane bucked through currents of heated air that spiraled up from the water as they skimmed islands and channels at treetop level.

Durell held a fully loaded AK assault rifle between his knees.

He had no way of knowing where Peta was, but his mind was on Leon. He remembered the Cuban's boast that he would destroy the dam in spite of security measures that prevented planting explosives on it.

The most obvious approach was by water.

He almost overlooked the barge. Fresh-cut brush covered it with mottled green from stem to stern, so that it merged with the waterscape—except that, unlike islands and drifting wood, it left a broad wake. The barge was big, perhaps fifty feet long, built in the forest-shielded secrecy of a backwater creek for only one purpose, Durell judged—and its hold, beneath the heaped rubbish that camouflaged it, would be packed with high explosives.

A steep bank, a sharp turn, and the Cessna roared over the barge low enough for Durell to snatch a glimpse of Leon's terrible face, the tiller by which he controlled a pair of large outboard motors, the abrupt lift of his machine pistol toward the Cessna—

And Peta in the bow.

Peta's Browning kicked, and the Cuban ducked before he could fire at the plane.

The two were at a standoff where one errant bullet would blow them both to bits.

Durell estimated the barge to be within three minutes of the dam, glanced that way, saw a hundred or more persons near a bunting-hung speaker's stand, their faces toward his plane as it dipped and circled.

His eyes slid back to the barge, and he saw that Leon would have to break away from the channels near the shore and make his final approach across open water. He considered detonating the explosives with gunfire. It would mean sacrificing Peta, maybe himself—concussion or debris might knock the airplane out of the sky. He could try to pick off Leon, but if a slug went astray, he thought grimly, the result would be the same.

In the end, he reminded himself, only the lives atop the dam mattered.

The wind screamed, and the engine whined as the plane came around, and Durell's desperation mounted as he became aware that this must be the last pass—the barge had turned out of the islands into the open lake.

Urgency thickened in his throat as he told the pilot to land.

The barge was no more than a minute from the dam when the Cessna's pontoons bumped against wavelets a few hundred yards away.

The machine pistol flamed in Leon's grip, and a grouping of watery feathers sprouted to starboard.

The Chinese pilot's thin, taut face leaned questioningly toward Durell.

"Ram it," Durell said.

The engine gunned, and the plane's red nose swung toward the dark, shaggy mass of the barge. Durell fastened his eyes on it, jaws clamped, a trembling hand on the shelf above the instrument panel.

He had chosen the best way he could think of to destroy the barge and still leave a margin of hope for survival—but it was not much.

He saw Leon's Stechkin yank, heard bullets snicker through the plane's skin, winced as the impact of a slug cracked a web in the windshield. His eyes switched to Peta as the distance narrowed swiftly, and he willed the stubborn youth to jump, but Peta hung on, trying for a shot at Leon.

The pilot's mouth hung open, and his breathing quickened, and his eyes jigged. He threw himself out the door.

Durell grabbed the controls, knowing only that the plane must not miss its target.

The bright air shook to the engine's roar, the pontoons' rumble, the spiteful thump of bullets. Blue and yellow flame spewed from the engine cowling; oily fumes curled into the cockpit. Another slug had damaged the controls, and the little Cessna fought Durell's hands now. The bucking wheel told him the flaming aircraft might veer off course if he left it too soon, and the dam would go, the country—a continent.

Only an instant was left to wonder if he could jump before it was too late.

Ahead, the coppery arc of Peta's body dived away. Durell saw the open hole of Leon's gaping mouth, his round black eyes, the shuddering Stechkin, then snakes of fire burst into the cockpit, blotting out everything, and Durell leaped free.

He cracked painfully against the water, arched up, saw through watery eyes as the flaming aircraft slammed into the barge. A monstrous hammer wracked his body, heat gushed over his face, and a volcanic bang joggled sky and earth.

The barge simply disappeared in a great cloud of fire and steam, and an enormous gray geyser hurling debris and mud blasted from the lake bottom soared high above the spot.

Echoes boomed and clattered through the Pakaraima hills.

Flocks of macaws squawked, swirled up from the trees.

The dignitaries watched from the dam in awed silence as the dirty mist of the geyser tumbled back into the seething lake.

The bow of a motor launch already hacked toward Durell and Peta, who treaded water a few yards apart.

"I am a man now," Peta called defiantly.

Durell was not moved to argue.

Chapter Thirty

Durell paused in the shade of the old breadfruit tree and regarded the sign that swung from rusty eyebolts over the entrance to Calvin Eisler's Georgetown shop.

A ribbon of memory, dim and unbidden, dragged behind his eyes, recalling the night before last when he and Ana, so eager to help, had narrowly escaped here with Eisler as their hostage.

He sighed, looked around. Traffic and shoppers crowded street and sidewalk. He still had ashes of the forest fire on his rumpled clothing, a long scratch across his cheek, but no one seemed to pay him any mind. The mingle of citrus and molasses scents from Stabroek Market, down the street, was strong in the early afternoon heat. The tradewind soughed in telephone wires, clashed with palm fronds and leaves of the breadfruit overhead.

The shops in the balconied arcade were busy—except for Guyana Exports.

Durell's eyes moved closely over faces in the crowd, then he strolled to the shop door. A hand-lettered cardboard sign gave notice that the establishment was closed for the remainder of the day.

He slipped toward the alley.

The police did not know he was back in Georgetown, and he wanted to keep it that way while he tested a theory or two, played out his hunches. Colonel Su's plane had flown him to Ruimveldt Seaplane Base on the south edge of town, and he had taken a taxi here. There had been no thanks or congratulations from dignitaries at the dedication. To them he had been only a small figure far down on the water, picked up hurriedly and, with Peta, hustled into the Chinese Canadair.

Colonel Su's discreet inquiries revealed that Eisler had flown Ana back to civilization as soon as she had arrived at the dam.

This time the white van was not parked behind Eisler's shop. Durell picked the padlock and let himself in. Memories of his desperate encounter here two nights ago swirled through his mind again as he worked his way out of the gloomy storeroom and into the shop area. The windows were closed, the air still and charged with an indefinable expectancy. Sweat popped out all over his body. He picked his way among the bubbling aquariums toward the piranha tank with its bloody tray of sliced liver and broomstraws. He became aware of a lingering taint of gunsmoke in the hot room, paused and listened. Beyond the window people walked and chatted. There was a soft, fountain quality to the babble of voices. Further away sunlight flared against chrome and glass, tires screeched. A traffic cop's whistle trilled.

Durell moved a few cautious steps, stopped once more, eyes dark and narrowed. Extending from behind the big tank was a foot clad in a white shoe.

Jan Browde's shoe.

Durell leaned and saw the extended body where it lay in deeper shadows. The hands and legs were tied, a wad of cloth stuck into the mouth. The blue eyes were big and round in the man's florid face. They blinked. The head wagged frantically, and muffled sounds came from behind the gag.

Durell stooped quickly, yanked the gag from his mouth, then worked on the knots.

Browde gasped for air. "Thanks, chum. I just knew it was Eisler, come back to finish me." Blood was caked around a hole in Browde's sleeve. He looked down at it and put his hand over it.

"Where is he?" Durell asked, unreeling rope.

"I don't know." Browde's face was going pale, and he looked faint. Durell saw that he had lost a lot of blood. Browde's voice was thin, as he said: "Eisler said he would throw me to the piranhas when he returned. I thought sure I'd bought it when I heard you."

Durell glanced into the tank. Most of the fish that had been there before were gone now. That did not surprise him. He turned back to Browde, and said: "Why did you set me up with Otelo Antunes' murder?"

"I didn't know about that, honest. Someone was using me, too."

"It was Eisler, of course. He's at the top of the diamond smuggling racket." He ripped the collar button from his shirt and said, "Look." He pressed the button into a piece of liver. Sticky blood held it there like glue. Then he chose a straw, thrust it through the liver, dunked it into the tank. A piranha instantly snapped the straw in two and swallowed liver and button.

"I see," Browde said. "He actually feeds diamonds to the little monsters."

"The fish are shipped to another country and killed and the diamonds retrieved," Durell said. "The idea came to me last night when I saw diamonds sticking to Claudius Gibaudan's bloody hand."

The two men stared at each other.

Browde broke the silence. "You're a cop, aren't you?"

"Not exactly—but that's close enough." Durell drew a Tokarev pistol that was Colonel Su's gift. "Now it's your turn," he said, his voice low and even.

Browde winced at the pain in his arm, licked sweat

from the corners of his mouth. "I guess I have to trust you," he said. "I'm an agent for the Central Selling Organization."

"South African. I should have known."

"A flood of illegal diamonds had been traced to Guyana. I was sent to find the leak in the dike. Had to work my way up from the bottom echelon boys. Then you came along with that brick of ice—"

"And we wound up working against each other."

Browde nodded weakly. "I set up the diamond deal in hopes of tracing the chain of buyers. After the killing of that reporter yesterday, everything dried up—I couldn't even find the people I'd been dealing with."

"What brought you here?"

"I got a tip just an hour ago that Eisler might be worth investigating. I came here, walked right into a trap."

"Eisler wanted to get rid of you as well as me," Durell said.

"He almost did," Browde said. He tried to shake the haze from his eyes, sucked a long breath between clinched teeth.

"I'll get an ambulance," Durell said, striding to the telephone. He made the call and unlocked the front door.

"Where are you going?" Browde called, his voice weak.

"I think I know where Eisler will be," he said.

The Grumman Gulfstream jet was a beautiful piece of machinery, Durell thought as he approached it in the crushing sunlight. It could fly fast and far—almost four thousand miles nonstop—and was much too expensive for shipment of a few gallons of tropical fish. Its sleek shape quivered behind curtains of rising heat, was mirrored in bright mirages that puddled the burning concrete and asphalt at a far corner of Timehri Airport's taxiways.

The white van was behind it, and Durell circled wide so that he could see that side of it, away from the airport tower, before going closer.

A thin angularity clambered up a metal ladder toward the airplane's door. That was Calvin Eisler, arms full with a container of tropical fish.

A jet liner swung out from the terminal building, thundering and screeching, found its runway, hurtled above the jungle that walled the airport all around.

Durell did not know if he had to do this. He wished to believe that local authorities could handle it—but Eisler was an important figure, the sort of man who had a way of landing on his feet, no matter what. He had Inspector Sydney James in his pocket, and there was no way of knowing how many others his money and position had corrupted.

Durell was almost in the shade of the plane, with the van between him and its fuselage, when Eisler took note of him. The tan of the tall, thin man's aristocratic face glittered with sweat, and he held a large container in his arms. He tried to smile. "I wondered what happened to you," he called down.

"I ducked the police," Durell said.

"And now you've come to fly out of our lives for good, I hope." Eisler made no move. The corners of his critical blue eyes were tight.

"Just to take you back to Georgetown," Durell said.

"I have my own transportation, thank you." Eisler's long teeth shone in a laugh. "Incidentally, I've dropped charges against you since the police recovered my car." He pronounced "car" like "caw."

"You killed Otelo Antunes, or had it done," Durell said bluntly. "You won't need your car for a long time."

"The sun must have got to your head," Eisler said.

"You were still trying to put me away, Cal. You were afraid I'd stumble onto your smuggling racket—that concerned you much more than exposure as a paid agent and ruination of your career. And I was the perfect suspect for Otelo's murder: the outraged brother-in-law, seeking revenge."

Eisler's eyes jerked toward the van. Durell had seen the feet on its other side. He thought he knew who was there.

Eisler's eyes came back to Durell, angry, squinting, threatening. "You're pushing your luck, Durell. Really."

"I'm used to that."

Ragged, broom-sized leaves hung listlessly under the raging heat along the verge of the airport as the two men measured each other. The jungle loomed behind a high chain-link fence, humming angrily. The memory of its muck and stings brought an abrupt shudder to Durell's heavily muscled frame.

An insipid current of air worried a lock of blond hair that dangled over Eisler's forehead. He still had not moved. Finally, he said: "You will never connect me with Otelo's death."

"Maybe not, for the record. It's enough for me that I know. You see, I noticed the aquarium fish in the log pits at that sawmill in Bartica—"

"Rather tenuous, Durell. Our country is noted for tropical fish in all its streams."

"But those would not have been there by choice. Characins prefer running water. Those had been penned there, waiting for you to pick them up. Peta confirmed that. It was sloppy thinking to choose your own property to frame me."

Eisler nodded toward a tank of piranhas that sat in the Grumman's door. "I should feed you to them for such insolent slander," he snarled.

"They're not interested." Durell's voice was bland. "Look at the little bastards—their guts are so full of diamonds they can hardly move."

A venomous gray changed Eisler's sky-blue eyes. He spoke calmly enough, as he said: "That does it. Kill him, James."

Durell had guessed that James' collusion had been all that made Eisler's control of the diamond pirates possible, and that he had been the man lurking behind the white van. He was not taken off-guard, had plenty of time, and the muzzle of his Tokarev awaited James' stocky form as the police inspector lunged from behind the van with drawn pistol.

Durell's gun made a flat, cracking sound, and James' beautiful brown eyes went dull and vacuous. He hit the tarmac a dead man, Durell's slug through his silk shirt, his heart.

Just then he heard Eisler's container splinter against the taxiway. He spun and crouched as Eisler's gun hammered wildly, was aware of the deadly suck of a bullet that whiffed past his ear. The Durell's Tokarev bucked in his fist, and a bruised blue hole opened at the base of Eisler's throat, and his jaw dropped, and the Tokarev crashed again. The second bullet took a shirt button into Eisler's chest. The man's arms flung out, and he fell amid bright spangles of fish that flopped under the brilliant sun.

Durell slowed his breathing deliberately, shook the tension out of arms and shoulders. He gave a tired grunt as he bent to pick up the spent 7.62 mm cartridges. Kneeling there, he twisted his head back toward the terminal, the hangars and freight warehouses.

The Grumman blocked them from his field of vision.

What happened here had gone unnoticed.

He turned and walked away.

Chapter Thirty-one

Chad Mitchell swiveled his chair around from the window as his willowy blond secretary showed Durell into his deeply carpeted office. The furnishings here befitted a rank two or three grades higher than Chad's, Durell thought, but that was all right. Chad would move up fast enough. In the meantime appearances were important to him.

"The warrior comes home," Chad said and extended his hand across the polished desk. He held a half-smoked cigarette in the other hand. He smiled beneath his impeccably trimmed mat of oiled yellow hair, but his moody brown eyes reserved their secrets.

Durell ignored the hand, sat down heavily across the desk from Chad. "Did you get Otelo's story suppressed?"

"I talked with the editor—"

"That's not what I asked."

Chad lifted a shoulder, as if his coat were binding him. "You know how it is with freedom of the press," he said. Then, apologetically, "We can't push too hard, Sam. We're not like you, in and then out. We have to live with these people."

"Still afraid to make waves," Durell rasped.

"So what? We've wrapped up the mission."

"Not quite."

"Okay. A few odds and ends, some reports. The embassy can truthfully say you've left the country by the time the papers hit the streets."

"Or shortly thereafter," Durell said. He made his face bland. "Maybe it's for the best."

"Sure. And get this: that Indian kid is over at Government House getting patted on the back—after we did all the work."

"I know. I took him there."

Durell glanced casually about the big office with its conference table and leather-upholstered sofa and expensive paintings. "You've reported the kernel of events to K Section headquarters, I presume."

"Yes." Chad sucked quickly on his cigarette. "And to the ambassador, of course. I'm afraid you stepped on a lot of toes, Sam. I tried to smooth it over. You'll apologize to the ambassador, now that it's all over—no point in leaving bad feelings to fester."

"No apology, Chad." Durell's tone brooked no argument.

Chad's eyes fell to his desk, then met Durell's gaze. "Very well, old man. No hard feelings between you and me, right?"

"Why should there be?"

"I don't care for your tone. Okay, we guessed wrong about Boyer—he hadn't been a careless fool, after all. And about the East Indians. Everybody makes mistakes, goddamn it."

"Your mistake might have cost me my life—it might have cost Guyana its freedom, not to mention the ultimate

179

price of revolution and conquest throughout South America."

Chad's yellow-stained fingers plucked angrily at his chin as the two men exchanged stares. Then he took a breath and said, "So you're pissed off." He dropped his voice and put an edge to his words. "I'll tell you something: I don't give a shit. I came out of this smelling like a rose, baby. You should see my report to the ambassador."

"Needless to say, you took as much credit as you could."

Chad gave a quick nod and grinned spitefully. "And there's nothing you can do about it. Write all the reports you like for K Section; mine is in State, and the twain shall never meet."

Durell just stared at the man, his eyes dark.

Chad said: "The prime minister called the ambassador to thank him for our help, after returning from the dam. The ambassador let me speak with him. I'm on my way, Sam, like it or not." He blew out smoke and added with a big smile: "I suppose you'd best be on your way, too. General McFee has informed us that a Miss Deirdre Padgett is waiting for you in Rio de Janeiro."

Durell felt a warmth that only the mention of Dee's name could bring, then Chad continued: "Your ticket to Rio is waiting at Timehri airport for you to pick it up."

Chad's eyes traveled over Durell's grimy clothing. "Before you leave, why don't you get a new suit? And take a shower, for god's sakes."

"So you've managed to take credit." Durell shrugged. "That's fine. You can take responsibility for the death of Eisler, too."

Chad's face paled. "You're joking."

"I had to kill him."

"For god's sakes . . . " Chad's thin jaw was hanging.

"And Police Inspector Sydney James. At the airport, half an hour ago. It's what I came to tell you."

"But—why? You son of a bitch!"

"I suppose there will be a hell of a stink," Durell said and rose from his chair.

"Surely there's an explanation!"

"Maybe. If the ambassador wants to read the K Section reports. He might get clearance in a month or two."

Chad stood up behind his desk. "You're not dropping this in my lap and walking out?"

"I'll send you a postcard from Rio," Durell said.

He strode through the door.

Watching the time carefully, Durell picked a blue suit from the rack in a small men's apparel shop, added a light blue tie with a woven pattern, white shirt, shoes, socks and underclothing, then returned to the Berbice Hotel for a steaming shower and shave.

He desperately wanted food and sleep, but there was time for neither, so he settled for bourbon and ice, brought by room service.

He carried his drink with him as he moved to the Demerara shutters, pushed them open and breathed deeply of the moist tradewind. His eyes ranged from the pink and white licorice-striped lighthouse to the distant seawall, the coffee-colored ocean beyond and back to the arcaded street below.

Down among the crowd of black and brown faces that drifted to and fro, newsboys had just begun shouting the day's headlines.

Durell sucked in a long breath and closed the shutters.

Chapter Thirty-two

Ana Morera was in a hurry.

She moved with long-stemmed grace among the smartly dressed urban dwellers and the country women in bandana turbans and calf-length cotton print dresses. As she turned into the sun on High Street, her face was the color of ripe grain, her eyes shadowed by a wide-brimmed straw hat beneath which she had piled her hair. She wore enormous rose-colored sunshades, a simple, deep-necked blouse of handwoven silk and a wide, free-flowing skirt of fawn material.

Calvin had called two hours ago and told her about the mysterious barge that had exploded near the dam after they had left there. It seemed he was always the first to know, as if he had a direct line to everywhere in the country. It would pay her to patch up their differences, once Sam Durell was out of the way.

She found it odd that she felt rather buoyant, considering what she had been through, what had happened in the jungle. But it was not as if anyone she'd really known had died out there.

Her life had been preserved.

So had Sam's.

It was as if fate had meant them to have this final moment together. Just them, after all the suspense and speculation, the labor and death.

She had not felt such elation since that time she'd sniffed coke in her dorm room. She had proven herself against the dare then, and again when she'd taken over her uncle's failing plantation and made it one of the most productive on the coast in three arduous years. Indeed, her short, successful life seemed to have been the conquest of one dare after another, from the time she had been orphaned as a small child, through a brilliant college career—and right up to today.

Something in the back of her mind quibbled against the chance she was taking, but her pride strangled the small voice before she could even begin to wonder.

Sam was brusque and self-contained and highly competent, she thought.

But he could be made to love her. And, if not, to desire her.

That would be enough.

She walked through the portals of the aging Berbice Hotel with a sense of confidence that was enhanced by the yearning stares that followed her swaying hips to the elevator. She smiled back through the closing doors from behind her sunglasses, then felt dimly alarmed at the passing giddiness.

That querulous little voice spoke again, asking if she knew herself as well as she had thought.

But of course she did.

There was a mirror in the elevator, and it told her that an almost imperceptible wisp of finespun hair had strayed. She pressed the strand back into place, then, in afterthought, ran the thin point of her pink tongue around her lips to make them shine.

She placed her sunglasses in her skirt pocket and studied her oval face. She must not look too eager. She took a deep breath, arched the neat lines of her black eyebrows, twitched her small mouth, then let her face fall back into place. Relax, she thought. Tiny stress lines disappeared from the corners of her eyes. The bell rang at the third floor.

If there was one thing for which she faulted herself as she stepped into the dusky hallway, it was waiting this long—but the pursuit, the test of wits, had been necessary to her ego, and she accepted that. She told herself that egotism was the necessary price of brilliance.

She curled her sharp little nose at the less than genteel fragrance of the Berbice and stood before Durell's door.

She took a moment to be delighted at the vision of his surprise, another second to run the soft flesh of her palm down her inner thigh. She smiled to herself.

Yes, it still was there.

The stiletto.

Durell had not reopened the window. The gloom was somehow comforting—fitting, he supposed, to his frame of mind. The air was hot, and the ice melted rapidly in its bucket. He took some of the hollowing cubes into his glass and filled it with bourbon. As condensation frosted the glass, Durell rubbed it across his forehead, aware of the wind slapping the window shutters. Pigeons cooed on the fire escape. A ship's horn mourned.

There came a knock at the door.

"Who's there?"

"It's me."

Durell unlocked the door, and Ana stepped in, smiling. She leaned back against the door to close it. Her eyes were the color of brass against fire, as she said: "I came to say good-bye."

Durell flicked the door latch, took two backward steps, hands at his sides. "You're right on time," he said.

"You were about to leave?"

"The papers just hit the streets."

"I should have brought you one. I came to give you something else." She closed the gap a step.

"I know," Durell said.

She was lovely, the wheaty sheaf of her neck a fine arch as her face turned up to him, the puffs of her perfumed breasts high against the low-cut blouse. Her eyes suggested intimacy; her lips expected a kiss. As she watched him, she tossed her hat onto a chair and unpinned her hair and it fell springy and black to her waist. Then her luxuriant body was a seductive pressure against his, the touch of her long thighs an invitation.

She made her voice low, and said: "Make this a special good-bye." Her lips met his with twisting eagerness.

Durell felt nothing, or, at least, not what she expected.

He made no response.

He decided there was little point in waiting, thought he might as well lay it all out.

She said, "Put your arms around me, darling."

And he said, "I ordered a background search on Leon Perez—only he wasn't Leon Perez, he was Martin Morera."

Ana's eyes flared beneath the dark wings of her lashes, and her lips parted slightly.

"Yes, Ana," Durell said. "Your father."

She did not release her embrace.

"He wasn't killed at the Bay of Pigs, was he?" Durell said. "He went there as a double agent for Castro, to betray the exiles and then rejoin Castro's people. And his face wasn't scarred in a volcanic eruption. It happened in that battle."

"Sam, darling—I don't want to talk about it." Her arms

184

tightened about his neck as she pressed her cheek against his shoulder. He felt her tremble a little.

"We have to talk about it, Ana. You'll have to do lots of talking."

Her fingers moved coolly across his chest and slipped a button of his shirt, then another. She hardly seemed to hear as Durell went on.

"Since the Bay of Pigs, your father had operated under deepest cover as an agent of the *Direccion General de Inteligencia*. We might never have traced him, but he was spotted in Africa, where he was instrumental behind the scenes in paving the way for the Cuban intervention in Angola. So many powers were in the shadows over there that he couldn't keep his role secret for long."

"Please, don't go on. We're all that matters now, just us." Her voice was pleading. Her lips touched the flesh over his heart.

"It's necessary that I finish, Ana. I hope you'll correct me where I am wrong. A formal statement will be necessary, of course." He lifted her chin with two fingers and spoke to her eyes. "The Cubans recruited you, with your father's help, in Spain last year. We know now that you were there at the same time—your name is on the passenger lists Dick kept in his files. They told you just to come back and get to know the right people, learn to be a good listener."

He was puzzled by the look in her eyes, and felt dimly annoyed by their frank, open stare, as if she thought that nothing he said could possibly make any difference.

"You won Eisler's confidence," he continued. "He had nothing to do with your operation, just as you had nothing to do with his. But he couldn't hlep boasting about the wealth of Claudius' diamond find—and you put your Cuban comrades onto the old man's trail. They took it over, then used the fear of the Warakabra Tiger to keep others away."

Ana's cool fingertips made little circles in the hair over Durell's breastbone. "It's so sordid, dear Sam. Can't we forget—for a little while?"

"I can't forget that you betrayed Dick, your old friend.

You were Otelo's source, Ana. You told him about Dick. And then about me."

Her reply was oddly detached, as if Durell were a ghost, and his words really did not matter. "Would I do that?" she said.

"You would, my treacherous little Ana. Only you and Chad Mitchell have used my code name here—and Chad is loyal, whatever other defects he might have. Otelo called me Cajun. He could only have learned it from you."

She kissed the middle of his chest and turned eyes the color of wild honey toward his face. "I didn't want you to be harmed—I hoped you'd leave the country. I wouldn't have done those things for anyone but my father."

"Maybe. But it was a challenge. You reveled in it. You threw up roadblocks everywhere. You were too arrogant to kill me—that wasn't exciting enough. You thought you could outsmart me."

Ana lowered her ear to Durell's chest. "Your heartbeat is so strong, so—vital."

"I'm afraid you're not quite well, Ana," Durell said. "We'll find a place for you, back in the States. You'll be interrogated, perhaps for weeks. There's much we don't know about the DGI. After that—"

It happened with stunning swiftness, in midsentence.

Durell did not see where the stiletto came from, only a flash of steel, a needlepoint—aimed at the smudge of lipstick that was like a target on his heart.

All his nerves popped, and his reaction was quick and instinctively savage. His arm flew out violently, crashed into Ana with triple the force necessary to knock her away, and, the next thing he knew, her slight figure was sprawled halfway across the room.

Her gasping breath sounded through the stillness, and her raven hair swung in a screen across her cheek as she raised herself on a shuddering arm, rolled onto her side. She pulled her knees up as if to cradle the handle of the knife that protruded from her stomach.

Durell dropped to her side, reached for the weapon. "No!"

Ana gave an agonized cough. Her hands clutched the silver handle and blood trickled and dripped from the tips of her fingers. Her lips skinned back from her teeth; her eyelids fluttered.

"I thought I could beat you," she gasped.

"I'm sorry, Ana. You were in over your head all the way."

She made a torn sound of rage and, with superhuman effort, jerked the blade from her body. She raised it to strike—but her eyes turned to muddy ice.

The stiletto clattered harmlessly to the floor.

Durell did not move for several seconds, his nerves ragged, his face wet with sweat. He regarded the body and thought how he could have proven nothing of Ana's complicity, even knowing that Leon was her father. He had not been certain that she was involved in the Cuban conspiracy until she came to his room to kill him. She must have known that even with his cover blown no one would blame the East Indians this time. Not after what had happened at the dam. But, as he had expected, her vanity had pushed her to this last desperate test; her intelligence had outwitted itself.

He dialed a number and wiped lipstick from his chest with the heel of his hand. When a highly placed aide in the prime minister's office answered, he glanced at Ana's face, stiffening with death.

"It's over," he said.

Chapter Thirty-three

Durell sat on the madras bedspread, hands hanging between his knees, as ambulance attendants covered Ana Morera's face and carried the stretcher out the door. The police had been informed through the office of the prime minister, just as they had been told of Inspector Sydney James and Calvin Eisler. In its present mixture of gratitude, alarm and urgency the government had given Durell a free hand and full backing for the completion of his assignment—although Chad Mitchell did not know this, and Durell was not about to tell him until the man had stewed awhile. Durell had not dared approach the police directly on his return to Georgetown—he'd had no way of knowing how deeply Eisler's corruption had penetrated.

Now the officers asked few questions, their tones deferential. They left with the sheeted corpse.

A dark, uniformed maid appeared with a bucket of suds and scrub brush. Durell watched through a daze of exhaustion as she scoured the blood from the floor. His head hung wearily from his shoulders, his body felt numb. When the maid left, he lay down just as he was, pulling his feet onto the mattress as if they were weighted with iron. His chest tingled where Ana's lips had touched, where the point of the stiletto had aimed.

He had two hours before the next plane left Timehri.

He felt as if he could sleep for a week.

About four o'clock Peta came in.

Durell shook the sleep from his eyes, ran fingers through his mussed black hair.

"I'm tired, too," Peta said.

"You know about Ana?"

Peta nodded, blew out a long breath, flopped in the old Morris chair. Pakaraima mud still smirched his shorts and sneakers. "I have been with men of the government. They told me. They made me eat with them."

"Was it so bad?"

"It was not good."

"I'm sorry about Ana," Durell said.

"She helped steal my father's claim. She would have killed me. You were right."

Durell could make nothing of the half-breed's green-eyed stare across the hot, gloomy room. The youth's hunting scars glistened in the low light. He still wore the beaded bands beneath his knees.

"What else did the government men tell you?" Durell asked.

"I will be rich. I will get a medal."

"That should make you happy."

"Yes. A medal is a rare thing."

Durell grinned. "I like you, son. Let's have a drink." He rinsed a tumbler and poured it half full of bourbon and handed it to Peta, then splashed a double into his own glass. They sipped in silence, Durell aware of the hollow mumble of Georgetown, the moaning whine of the unceasing wind.

After a minute had passed, Peta said: "If I am rich, I can build a new shack."

"Yes."

"And buy Miss Morera a big tombstone, a pretty one of pink rock."

"If you wish, Peta. There will be money left over."

"You can have some of my money. As much as you like. Take the big diamond. They said I would get it back."

"You keep it," Durell said. "Perhaps you can use it to help your tribe."

"They have the forest and rivers." Peta looked sad. "The government men said my life will change. What do you think?"

"I'm afraid they are right," Durell said. "You should prepare yourself for it; use some of your money for lessons; go to college one day. You'll be a big man."

"I am a man already."

"Oh, yes."

"I want to be a man like you. You have respect. You know guns and fighting."

"That doesn't make a man, Peta. Only deep convictions and the daring to stand up for them."

"Would you teach me those things?"

"I couldn't," Durell said, and smiled at the troubled furrows that crowded Peta's brow. "But you already have them," he added.

Peta looked proud. Then the rangy youth rose and held out his hand, and Durell took it, and they stood, each with a hand on the other's shoulder. A picture flashed across Durell's mind: Peta in Prince John with him and Deirdre, learning the skipjack. But Peta was not meant for those cold and complex northern climes; his place was here. Durell did not think wealth would spoil him, and he saw no fear of the future in those bright jade eyes.

"I'll go now," Peta said. "Thank you, Mr. Durell."

"Call me Sam."

Peta's grin was a surprise of broad, flashing teeth. "Maybe we will meet again," he said.

"I'd like that."

As the big jet winged toward Rio, the memory of Ana blunted Durell's satisfaction in the job just completed. He had not thought she would have to die. Leon had used her callously, and for an orphan to succumb to the will of a father returned from the grave was an understandable sin, however vile. Durell sighed, gazed at the darkening horizon, and the hours dragged by until, at last, the airliner thumped down at Galeao International Airport that night.

Durell's spirits did not begin to lift until he checked in at the sumptuous Hotel Pao de Acucar. The life flowing back into him had nothing to do with the blazing sweep of Copacabana Beach with its splendid *Carioca* girls, nor the vital throb of bossa novas and sambas that spilled from countless nightclubs and discos.

He knew that Deirdre waited for him here, in this hotel, and her presence was almost palpable through the din and dazzle.

When they met in their room high above the city, with Sugarloaf and the ocean beyond their balcony, nothing more than, "Dee . . . " would pass the tightness in his throat.

"Sam—oh, Sam!"

She dropped a book she was reading and threw her arms around him, and he felt a slight tremor in her tall frame with its intelligent gray eyes and mantle of embered black hair. He kissed her and leaned back, holding her patrician shoulders in both hands. In her eyes he saw the calm serenity that was her anchor against all the deadly currents that swept them.

They did not speak for a long moment as their gazes mingled and they held each other close.

Durell thought briefly of what life might be if he never returned to K Section, then shrugged it away. And there were thoughts, as he held her with accustomed intimacy, of strong sons and beautiful daughters—an ambition that seemed modest enough when you looked around. But he put that out of his mind as well.

His job was his only purpose in life, and he did not see that changing.

Then Deirdre led him toward the bed with, "Come here, darling Sam."

And he decided he could only make the most of what he had.

That was quite a lot.